# Ports of Entry

# Ports of Entry

*Love ya brotto!*

Jeremy Schewe

Inchanted Journeys Publishing

2018

# Ports of Entry

Copyright © 2018 Jeremy Schewe

First Printing: 2018
Printed in the United States of America
First Paperback Edition

Cover Design: Jeremy Schewe
Cover Art: Neva Morgan Lockamy
Edits to "Oweynagat na Rath Cruachan" by Alexander Tait

ISBN 978-1-387-62876-6

Inchanted Journeys Publishing
18 Woodridge Lane
Asheville, North Carolina 28806

www.inchantedjourneys.com

Ordering Information:

Special discounts are available on quantity purchases by corporations, associations, educators, and others. For details, contact the publisher at the above listed address.

U.S. trade bookstores and wholesalers:
Please contact Inchanted Journeys Publishing
Tel: (828) 505-1630; or
email jeremy.schewe@gmail.com

# Dedication

Twenty-one years ago, in the not-so-quiet hovel of a college dorm room, amongst the weavings of dreams and unfolding magic, *Ports of Entry* opened for interchange. I dedicate this book to Tracy of Floyds Mound, Indiana, because she was there when the ports first opened and requested the honor. I have not forgotten you.

I also offer my gratitude for the fruition of this book to Miss Sunwater, the Morrigu, the Valkyrie, the Irish Orchid, the Pythea, and Nineveh. Our passions shaped me in the muses' forge of love, desire, and inspiration. And most of all, I wish to thank Kalia, the Bear, for your love, devotion, teeth, and claws. I thought I knew what loyalty and passion were until I decided to share my den and open the portals to care for this temple with you.

Finally, I offer this book to the dreamers and visionaries who are initiating tangible change in our world. I would also like to honor all those who are tracking their heritage and ancestral lines back to their source - to a place of belonging and to the stories within that seek to rise again wriggiling and writhing with life force.

The more ways we

Weave our stories,

The more we weave ourselves

Back together again.

There is no original story.

Our first life breath

Many eternities ago

Is the original story.

We are all re-weaving

The pieces of one great story

Back into a whole.

Every storyteller knows this.


Delfina Rose, <u>Star Song Oracle</u>

# Contents

# Preface

The stories and prose in *Ports of Entry* are living mythology. These are not stories that you will find in traditional tales or a book, though some of the characters will be recognized by readers. The stories herein are what may occur when we are invited into firsthand experiences with often unexplainable phenomena through our imagination, intuition, vision, ceremony, or suffering. In these firsthand experiences, we are invited to "step through the veil". The veil could be as simple as a worldview or limiting belief. It may be a life-changing experience like death, marriage, divorce, an accident, or witnessing the power of a miracle like birth, compassion, or love. In religious or spiritual mystery traditions, the veil is the threshold that bridges the human world with the spirit world. The veil can provide a temporary doorway that connects linear time to timelessness, or a port of entry. Latin American *curanderos* know it as *la época de mito,* where past, future and present mix together. The Irish Celts know it as *Tír na nÓg*, or the blessed realm of the eternal youth.

The purpose of this book is not to prove to academia or even to the casual reader that spiritual mysteries are alive and well in the world. I know that they are fully alive and well, though they hunger to know us each individually. *Ports of Entry* as a book is instead a sharing of semi-tangible experiences where the veil has been crossed with intention or by happenstance. Most often, a mystery shows up uninvited, knocking loudly at the door and demanding a cup of tea or something to eat. In other words, uninvited interactions request that we pay attention to something that has been seeking our ministrations. The mysteries open us up to the majesty of life. They rekindle a sense of awe and wonder.

Mysteries appear to us exactly in the way that we can best perceive. One person may witness in vision an ancient god or goddess, while another may see Christ or Mother Mary, while still another may see angels or star beings at a Galactic Council. It has been one of my primary goals in life to become a translator of vision.

And more so, it has been my intention to connect with the mysteries of a region through the eyes of the indigenous or local culture. This is not always the easiest task as our brains have been programmed for our entire lives to see things within our own cultural context.

I have had the honor of working on many conservation or ecological restoration projects around the world. Lengthy immersion in indigenous and regional cultures, connected deeply with the regional ecology, and a healthy respect for local lore and mythology often have provided an excellent opportunity to observe and listen. Each experience is an invitation to change perspective and perhaps even change how the world looks, or in other words change how we believe the world looks.

Imagine a camera with multiple lens attachments. Each lens tightened onto the camera captures images in respect to how the lens bends light into the camera and records that image. The development or the graphic image can be enhanced on the backend to manipulate the image, or to portray a story that viewers may gain some perspective or illumination from. Our "lenses" are our beliefs. Our beliefs are developed from years of indoctrination and environmental conditioning. Global conservation work has enabled me to gather a few more lenses. It is through these lenses that I "see" the mysteries through a local set of eyes.

The stories and characters of *Ports of Entry* are derived from many mythological traditions including Celtic, German-Nordic, Greek, Assyrian, Native American, Polynesian, and others, but are by no means limited to these traditions. Within each of these cultures, and the powerful and sacred lands that they traditionally inhabited, are the roots, stems, flowers, fruits, and seeds that have been nurtured, sustained, oppressed, crushed, forgotten and remembered again and again across millennia. The stories are snippets in an initiate's interaction with allies and foes while climbing the world tree in their respective indigenous and cultural traditions. Each of these cultures sustains a world tree, or *axis mundi* around which their spiritual and secular culture flourished. The trees penetrate the worlds and connect the celestial with the Earth. Thus, as one climbs the cultural and mythological tree of their ancestors or dream line, it awakens deeper states of cognizance as greater perspective is obtained and a sense of wonder augmented.

Suppose we could climb a tree together. Let us start from a gentle walk in Central Park, or even better, let us have someone drop us from a helicopter into the deep bush of Australia, the headwaters of the Amazon, the cloud forests of Guatemala, or in an ancient forest along the rocky coast of British Columbia. We will find some mighty trees to ascend. Start we should with the basics: climbing gear and physical proficiency. Then, we will study the shape of each trunk and set our ropes accordingly. After a safety crosscheck, we begin to climb while observing everything about where we place our hands and feet. Perhaps we will have the opportunity, if we do not climb too fast, to witness the varying creatures and beings that inhabit the strata as we climb.

Some climbers may want to spend days on one tree. Some may want to spend weeks or lifetimes there. Some climbers go up and down as fast as they can and move on to the next. Yet, there are those who would bring multiple ropes and fasten them to stout branches in the canopy and swing through the forest from tree to tree, observing, witnessing, experiencing and gathering along the way. There is no correct way to experience the climb.

Some trees have guardians who know every secret there is about their respective tree. Yet, they often cannot see beyond their own spectacles to see the forest for the rest of trees. There are those who know the forest floor and those who know the canopy. There are those who know how to grow trees and those who know how to shape them into something new. There are those who know the trees' medicine and those who know how trees are taxonomically related. And there are also those who only stop to enjoy the fruits and nuts, or to chase a butterfly, or to get caught in a snare.

In the Celtic tradition, druids were the guardians of the trees. As keepers of lore and knowledge, some druids were like lawyers, doctors, or priests of today. Many druids were like professors of today's colleges and universities, or their research assistants and post-doctoral researchers. Individuals tended to a certain school of thought or tree of knowledge in the forest of the mind, such as herbology, architecture, astronomy, geology, economics, metallurgy, martial arts, and so on. Each field of knowledge corresponded to a tree species. Thus to be a guardian of all knowledge, a druid was a guardian of the entire grove.

So come and pull down a story from the canopy of the infinite library of the sacred grove. Climb the world tree of another culture and see what you find in its branches. The stories in *Ports of Entry* do not need to be read in any certain order. The stories herein come from the hunting of the Wyrm of the Earth, the Cosmic Serpent, or the Tao. The hunt grants the hungry reader an opportunity to draw down living, wiggling stories from the canopy, the trunk, or the roots of a world tree at a port of entry, and wrestle them into a form that someone else can discern. Depending on their level of craft, perhaps they can blend the essence of the heart of creation, fuse it with the elemental, and bend the probabilities to rewrite the past, future, and present. Stories catalyze the arcane as they undulate through the plains of consciousness; and, sprout new life for our indigenous mysteries to take on new life and thrive in the modern world.

*Ports of Entry* is organized roughly into cultural groups of which the stories are derivatives. It is my hope that the following pages will come to life for you. It is my wish that the stories will not altogether behave themselves by staying on the paper, but will instead leap up off the pages wiggling and squirming to life in your mind's eye. And even more so, it is my hope that you will remember somewhere along the way where you had a similar experience. Then perhaps you will accept these tales as an invitation to listen to your dreams or the beckoning of standing stones to come home. Follow the trail out your door to burial mounds and quartz encrusted cliffs. Hungrily seek out waterfalls, deep forests, and caves. I hope to stimulate your appetite enough to seek out the wilds of this world on your own. Follow the trail that leads you on. It is your life. It is your skin bag of water, blood and bones. It is your body, animated by none other than the greatest mystery of all: life.

Perhaps you will discover the tree of your ancestors waiting to germinate and grow in good soil. Perhaps you will find a forgotten port buried under hundreds of meters of ocean. Perhaps you will find some nugget of goodness tucked in the hollowed out bole of an old oak. Stretch your branches into the cosmos and burrow your roots into the bones of the Earth. One day we will meet in the shade of a great banyan, cedar, or beech tree, and exchange stories, pleasantries, and news of the world before we swing on to the next story. I will see you there. Beyond the reach of the Digital god, there is a deep, primordial essence that is looking for you as it was once looking for me.

# First Nations

# Blue Heron's Husband

Wind yourself down and have a seat by the fire. When your bones are sitting comfortably upon the cushion of your backside and you can hear the breath of the Creator in the heart of a whelk's chamber, I will tell again the story of how my brother became the Blue Heron's husband. This is a story of quietness that cannot be heard with loud ears, though if loud ears are all that arrive by way of the fire tonight, then I will do my best to share the telling in a way that invites you to shake the crust from your mind.

Please, do have a seat. I will invite you to lay down your cares at the shores of Turtle Island, and let the waves smooth them into nothing until you are a child again. There now, soften the brow and open the heart. Invite again the weeping and singing for pure innocent joy in the beauty of creation. Roll in the sand if you must. Then we can walk together for a few miles down the sandy beach and listen to the sea birds arguing over crab legs. Let the wind and sun kiss us gently until we are golden brown.

To the west, over the dunes crowned with coppered sea oats, is the salt marsh that my brother and I used to frequent as young boys. When the tide was in, we would hide in the tall sea grass, waiting for fish to swim among the reeds. When the tide was out, we would tiptoe in the muck between the oyster colonies, pretending to be mighty hunters looking for the Crab King. But best of all were the days we crept quietly over the dunes from the beach through the sea oats, careful not to put our hands and knees on the prickly pear cacti, to where we could silently observe the fisher birds in the estuary. On most mornings, the egrets or cranes stalked about in their jaunty silence. Yet, on mornings where the golden magic of sunrise would elevate our hearts to the pureness of freedom and exploration, we could observe our favorite huntress, the Blue Heron.

We could watch the Blue Heron for hours. Often, we would just sit and watch her, while other times we would unobtrusively mimic

3

her movements in the sea grass. First, we would begin with our arms, then our necks, and soon our whole bodies, moving silently and slowly in her image. The moving rhythm of the heron was a mystical charm bestowed upon our innocent hearts and minds. As she moved through the still water, the rhythm of her steps went like so:

"Da, dee-da. Dee-da, ka-da, da. Dee-da. Ka-da pa, pa-pa-ka-dee-pa. Da, kee-da."

And so on. Sometimes the rhythm would move faster and sometimes slower. The more she moved, or the less, the more we strived to sway in the miming dance. We were completely enraptured in her beauty and poise. We were timeless perfection. During some spells, the entire day would be lost in our trance and dance. The setting sun, over the scrub-maritime forest west of the salt marsh, would steal a look at us before disappearing for the day, as if to remind us in a condescending manner that we were missed at home.

As we grew older, we would imagine that the Blue Heron was the mostly lovely woman in the universe. As we watched her grace unfold, she slid perfectly across the glassy surface of the brackish seawater. Our hearts imagined her form changing from a great bird into the absolute perfection of woman's beauty. The slightest change in the lighting, or shaking our heads lightly, and the vision would be dispelled.

My brother said to me once with a sparkle in his eye, "Someday, I am going to ask her to be my wife."

I was never sure what to say to that. It is a facetious place in the mind, encompassed in the quietness of a wild place, which can be at loss for words that do not really need to be spoken. I just smiled.

One of our grandmothers used to tell us stories about her home in the west of Ireland, out where the sea would break on boulders and cliffs. As a young girl, she was often privy to things that young lads were not, especially in respect to things of a feral nature and unseen realms. She would transfix us with tales of entire worlds underneath a

4

cairn, or different worlds opening when walking through standing stones. The stories that always stuck with my brother and me were the tales of the Selkies. And if you do not recall the Selkie stories that I have shared with you on other nights by this fire, then I will have to ask you to hold your tongue for the moment. We can revisit one of those on another night.

As my brother and I grew into young men, our pursuits in the world began to diverge. I was interested in running the family farm and my brother became more enraptured by the world around us and became, if anything, a naturalist and poet. While I worked the farm and courted pretty ladies, my brother became more reclusive and spent ever further time wandering the wild country, the salt marshes, and the beaches.

At times, he would make it home to have dinner with the family, but a continuously more feral look grew within his eyes as time passed - almost like a wild creature that does not belong within walls or under a roof. He was good mannered enough, though the slightest wind cutting across a window pain, or the rattling of the wooden gate to the yard, would cause him to fidget uncomfortably in his chair as if he was held in the family home against his will. Alas, his discomfort could not be gratified until he was outside under the open sky once more.

He was not inclined to join in conversation in those latter years. Often it seemed that he had traded his gift of speech for the eloquence of the natural world. It is not that he could no longer speak; it was that words were cumbersome burdens in the pathway of communicating anything of true interest. He would trip over words with his tongue, for they never seemed sufficient to convey his experience. Yet birds would light upon his shoulders with a gentle call from his parsed lips. Driftwood or woven reed mats he brought home from his wanderings were scattered around the home and yard in plenty, and though his words infrequently were shared, these crafts of his hands spoke eloquently of the beauty of creation.

ɔΨϲ

My brother came home during a pouring rain that often comes at the tail end of hurricane season. Mom and Dad were in their later years. Grandmother had passed on a few years back, and my wife and two young girls were the life of the table now. My brother stumbled into the house, after weeks away from home, and his eyes were filled with light. He sat down at the table. I noticed he no longer had his shoes. His pant legs were tattered beyond all repairs.

As I passed the soup around the table toward him, he looked at me. Well, it would better said that he looked through me, straight to my heart, melting all the years between us until we were both little boys playing again on the dunes. I could taste the salt air on my tongue and found my breath wedged in my throat. The oyster middens heap of our ancestors flashed before my eyes. There we were, miming the Blue Heron on a warm afternoon, deep in the salt marsh.

"I have seen her," said he. "She is going to be my wife."

A perfection of form, both of heron and woman, danced almost visibly between us like a ghost between the gateways of our eyes. I could hear the drum of my heart pulsing in my veins.

"Da, dee-da. Dee-da, ka-da, da. Dee-da. Ka-da pa, pa-pa-ka-dee-pa. Da, kee-da."

In the back of my mind, the melody of a gentle flute took the shape of sea gulls, bellies white to the sun. Their black wings stretched to span the beach and look for good things to eat. Sea oats rustled in the breeze sweeping over the dunes from the south, hissing at the pulsing surf and claiming the loose sand as terrestrial domain for a few more cycles of the earth around the sun.

There she was, dancing. She was perfection. Her poise was sharp-roundness. She was grace unfolding. The lines of her legs, arms, and finger tips could touch the limitless horizon and beyond, almost as if she was the center of the universe, directing the casting of the symphonic web. My heart began to weep in longing and the knowledge that such beauty could be part of this world. I felt the years crack off of me like dried marsh muck and there was my brother, clear-eyed looking back at me.

He smiled. He smiled like I remembered him, many years ago, with a knowing. There is nothing that could be said or should have been said. I passed him the soup.

That was the last time my brother ever came home for dinner. To this day, I do not know where my brother has gone. But the Blue Heron knows, I can guarantee it. When he did not come home for over a full cycle of the moon, I went looking for him. I knew where to go, for the last gift he gave me was the return of innocence, and thus mental clarity. With my blinders thus removed, I walked down the beach slowly, collecting shells and listening to the voice of the Creator within the crashing waves. When I arrived at what had once been our secret passage over the dunes to the salt marsh, I stole a look at the heavens. In that instant, a single sea gull careened its head to the west, peering down upon me before disappearing to the south along the shoreline.

I stepped over the sea oats and prickly pear, and crept slowly down to the marsh on all fours. It did not take long to see her. The Blue Heron was moving with perfection through the surface of the glassy water.

"Da, dee-da. Dee-da, ka-da, da. Dee-da. Ka-da pa, pa-pa-ka-dee-pa. Da, kee-da."

I began to mimic her as my brother and I did in our youth. My right arm, at first became her neck; and, my hand, her head. My hand looking for fish and crabs among oysters and reeds. My feet began to slide into the dance soon after, until my whole body was again a heron on the hunt. I followed her movements gently as the sun passed its zenith. In this short-shadow time, two things happened simultaneously that have forever changed the way I move in the world.

First, I heard the primordial call of another Blue Heron, her mate. He called out again, sailing over the glassy water of the marsh with a six-foot wingspan landing assuredly in the water adjacent to her. For a moment, they seemed to exchange pleasantries in a quiet fashion, before the hunt continued in silent tandem.

Second, I put my bare feet down on something quite soft, but not natural. I was pulled instantly from my reverie to find that I was standing on weathered, sandy clothing. My pulse quickened as I stooped down to look at the articles more closely. My stomach sank. They were my brother's. I recognized the shredded slacks from the dinner that we had shared together as our last super.

An entire moon had passed since I saw him last. There were no footprints leading toward the clothing or away from them. Many rains and afternoon breezes had seen to the obliteration of any other traces of my brother's course. I was torn even further from my reverie, when I realized how much time had been lost from my search for my brother in the timeless heron dance I had entered. I had forgotten about my brother entirely.

That is when I heard the sound of the male Blue Heron call like an ancient Pleistocene beast, rippling across the estuary. I looked out to the water, still as glass, where two herons moved in precision around oysters and reeds.

"Da, dee-da. Dee-da, ka-da, da. Dee-da. Ka-da pa, pa-pa-ka-dee-pa. Da, kee-da."

Intuition and knowing washed over my fear, like loving hands over a tired and sore body. My heart was filled with profound peace.

To do this day, I am not really sure what happened to my brother. But if you have even a fraction of a percentage of the Good Folk coursing through your blood, or you happen to be blessed with the eyes of innocence or second sight, you know where my brother is, as do I.

There are some that say that if you have the inkling, rise before the sun. Make your way north along the shore and cross the dunes, passing through the sea oats and prickly pear. Move quietly and with precision down amongst the reeds to where the water is glassy in the moonlight, and wait. Wait until the sun crests over the sea and her golden fingers crawl over the dunes. Wait there in the reeds hidden until the golden fingers warm the back of your ears.

You may see the Blue Herons hunting in the marsh. They will be dancing. She is perfection. His poise is sharp-roundness. She is grace unfolding. The lines of their legs, arms, and finger tips could touch the limitless horizon and beyond, almost as if they were the center of the universe, directing the casting of the symphonic web. For a moment they will be birds, for a moment humans. My heart will always weep in joyous gratitude, knowing that such beauty is part of this world.

# How the Daddy Long-Leg Got his Long Legs

At a time when the world was young and the grasses and flowers' songs still were audible to any listening ear, Grandmother Spider and Grandfather Spider were one of the First People to dwell on Turtle Island. Both were excellent hunters who kept their tribe fed and well protected. Grandmother was a weaver of webs of probability, and Grandfather was a seeker and jumper. Grandmother Spider was well known for the intricacy and beauty of her webs. Whatever silky lines of unknowing she would cast into the universe; they would always connect to another thread with resilience. She would rest at times in the center of her web and listen for songs on the winds of chaos, and the nourishment that they would bring to her. She captured some of those songs and brought the feast of music to her tribe and family.

Now Grandfather Spider did not take the time to cast webs as his wife. Grandfather did not have the patience or the skill at the craft of weaving. Grandfather's craft lay in his natural ability to stalk, leap, and ride the currents of chaos of the then young world. Like a hunter masterfully steering a canoe in a great northern river, Grandfather Spider would ride the wind currents to land on the very backs of his quarry.

For many a lifetime in the contemporary sense of things, Grandmother and Grandfather lived in this way. She wove webs, channeling chaos into order and manifestation of life's sustenance. He rode the waves of chaos as a surfer and caught what he chose instead of waiting for it to come to him. For many a life-time they lived in happiness, each to their own craft, or at least until Grandmother's web caught a newcomer to the world, a being which we now know as a dragonfly. Her catch fed the tribe for weeks.

Our fine spider couple had always been a bit competitive, but this catch of Grandmother's was too much for Grandfather Spider. He had been chasing dragonflies since they had squeezed between the lips of the mouth of the Creator and emerged in the East, where the great twin rivers become infinite freshwater swamps. He had had little success, always settling for easier catches such as flies and mosquitoes. So to say the least, Grandfather grew quite jealous of this new development and began devoting his time to capturing larger prey. But capturing larger prey meant that the victims were stronger and more difficult to hold onto. With each catch, his legs were stretched further and further, stretching his skin tighter and tighter, and straining his small body to where it became smaller and smaller. Soon his mouth was able to open less and less, while his food became more and more.

This continued until one day he snared the ultimate prey: a human child. The child ran and screamed, trying to throw Grandfather off, but to no avail. The child rolled and scraped its arms on trees and rocks, but to no avail. Grandfather would not let go. Yet, in the meantime his legs were stretched so thin that his mouth could barely open and he could not quite bite his prey.

Finally, he let go, but his legs were permanently stretched almost beyond use other than to tiptoe around the forest floor. And his mouth was so tiny that all he could do was lay by a stream and cry and cry. Cousin Copperhead heard his tears, and feeling sorry for Grandfather, slithered up the stream to comfort and comfort. He offered some of his venom as a condolence for Grandfather's bereavement, which Grandfather put into red amber bags that he could tie onto his legs, such long legs. These venom bags could be bitten open by Grandfather Spider during a hunt to poison his prey so that he could still hunt and honor his people, for his mouth was too small to capture most anything delicious.

To this day, before the sun leaps up from the Underworld in the east, Grandmother Spider morns and morns the misshapen nature of her husband. Her tears can be seen dripping from her webs as the first light of the sun illuminates their strands, circling, circling. Waiting for another song to be sung, she is watching for the probability of her husband's glory to be restored.

# The Ghost of Nothing

---

Ing. Some say that he is a giant. He lives there alone, you know, at the edge of all things considered civil. He has a medicine bundle dangling from his hip that contains the universe. Reaching inside, one might find roots, flower petals, bits of bark, a stone, or an odd feather. Yet reach a little deeper and find a colony of wind riders, a rook of blue herons, or an entire forest of butterflies.

I once had the honor of meeting this wild giant, there at the edge of all things civil. He smiled at me, keeping his distance as he rummaged through a patch of stinging nettle. I approached him in the way that my Grandmother and the Lady Erin had taught me when I was wearing the dream-skin of my youth. I set all of my thoughts down under a white oak to be gathered later. I emptied my cask of stagnant water by the trout lilies under a beech tree; drew a gem from the embers of the lodge fire in my heart; and, placed it there among the understory of goldenseal.

I presented the gem in a sanctuary where the worms could not get to it, yet within Ing's line of vision, there by the wake robin, larkspur, and bloodroot, on a tuft of clubmoss. And I sat in silence, watching the hawthorn berries ripen. It is an interesting place, to allow the mind to become a river, and to slip between water and sky and earth. Along the shores of the mind, worlds are born and die, and dreams are thick and palpable. One can almost taste the expanse of the universe, while the breath becomes the infinite ebb and flow of the sea.

Ing's interest was perked after the procession of equinoxes trickled by through the ages. I could feel his gaze navigate between my heart and the gem, piercing, yet surging through me like a strong wind in the canopy of a pine forest. He stole a side glance at the nettles, weighed his decision, and despite his vast magnitude, gracefully bridged the gap between us to collect the offering.

13

He drank in the story of the gem through the veil of his fingers and skin, there at the edge of all things civil. He listened intently to the resonance within the gem and for a moment, traveled through it with his immortal soul like a hunter in his canoe crossing a great river. A silent pause in the turning of the universe stilled the forest, longer seeming than the life of a hundred ravens, before his great green eyes flashed up at me smiling. There was unfathomable quietness there. Quietness deeper than any well or the vastness of any sea, and it pulled at the very essence of my being. Through those eyes, I was being drawn into the emerald eternity of primordial forest that was free of the grip of time - where tree songs still swam in the currents of the earth, springing from stones, rivers, mountains, and fantastical creatures. The forest within his eyes was thick. I found myself immersed in the wilds with little to orient myself to a sense of place. I lost the pathway of my soul, slipped on moss-covered logs, and banged my knee on the knobby limbs of a hickory.

He emerged from this forest, there in the shadow of no-thing civil. From the slip between shadow and light he came, like the sunrise he was masked in mist and fire. I could not stand up to meet him, for my legs were soft as if my bones had turned to pudding. He danced, throwing cloaks from the mantle of my mind, pulling demons and poison from my limbs with his song. He sucked the fear from the very marrow of my bones until I was naked and he satiated. He tore away my identity, my spine, my "me", that I too could swim into the perpetual currents of the earth.

I let go.

I do not know where I went. Going somewhere indicates a destination outside of self and creation. Those boundaries and constructs were conquered by this ghost-of-nothing.

Ing.

I hear his thunder drums call.

Ing.

My flesh is the laughter of the mountains whose single breath is a thousand human generations.

Ing.

I know that you are still here amongst us. I hear you calling in the night.

I still find the doorways when I empty my cask just so, and polish a gem within to offer to a Keeper with care. I pick up my thoughts from the base of the white oak, and hold the hand of the beech when she allows it. I did reach into Ing's medicine bundle that day. First, went my hand, then my arm... until my entire being was consumed by the timeless confines of that satchel. I found no-thing there, only nudity and an empty vessel ready to sail the firmament. There is nothing more that I could want, so I sing, here at the edge of all things civil.

And Ing? Hmmmmmm... I imagine he is collecting nettles in the rich coves if you would like to reach into his bundle.

# Oshawa: The Forgotten People - Where is Our Rice?

Sometimes I could hear them at night. On nights when the moon was ripening and the black lakes were still. I could hear their cries slicing through chilled North Country air. I would be dreaming of wild rice and blueberries, great log jams on icy lakes waiting for the spring, and wolves curled around one another in their dens. The cries in the night would rip me from my slumber, and I would be left naked, as the mantle of sleep would slide off of my bed and leave my mind sharp, crisp, and alive.

Then I would listen. Silence met me in stillness.

The cry came again; a piercing cry that sent chills up and down my spine like fingernails on a chalkboard in an arctic blizzard, leaving my hairs standing at attention. The cry echoed around the lake of my mind like a ghost, whispering, "Where is our rice?"

"I don't know," I think. "Where is your rice? Perhaps you mean wild rice?"

I hear the crying again, "Where is our rice?"

"Perhaps you should ask the Voyageurs or the boatmen," came the thought to my mind, "or the miners and timber barons."

"Where is our rice?"

Their cries continued to echo through the boreal forest and across glacier carved lakes in granite. Outside, the aspen, birch, and spruce whispered things to the wind in a forgotten language. I dressed quickly and made my way down the stairs for the door.

"I am coming," I thought.

"Where is our rice?"

17

I stepped across the threshold into the outer world and allowed my eyes to adjust to the bright moonlight.

"Where is our rice?"

Threading my way through the bracken ferns and sarsaparilla toward the granite outcrop that looked over the lake, my hands pressed against the moonlit bark of birch and directed me clear of the dark spruce. The familiar scratching of low-bush blueberries on my legs told me when I was getting close to the outcrop.

"Thank you, my friends, for pointing the way," I would say as the canopy of the forest would open to the glowing granite in the moonlight.

"Where is our rice?"

Yes, the rice. Well, this outcrop was a meeting place where worlds folded over one another. The Ojibwa, or Kojejewininewug, used to trade with the Oshawa on this location before time caught up with them. The French-Canadian Voyageurs once traded here as well with the Ojibwa. The Oshawa has had very few people to trade with over the last 100 years, as few recognize the fold in the universe that the Oshawa nation dwells within.

"Where is our rice," the Oshawa ask, persistently to any who can listen.

For years, whenever I heard their calling, I would sit up straighter in whatever northern company I happened to be in, wondering who it was that needed the rice. I stopped asking after a while because I kept getting unacceptable and varying answers. The lilt of the northern tongue would leave me with…

"Oh! No one said a thing!"

"Oh, yah, that was just a loon on the night lake. Want some more Walleye?"

"Nighthawks you heard, a night hawk, see?"

18

Or a bittern.

Or a cougar.

Or someone's house boat engine idling. I still to this day, have not found anyone from the North Country or otherwise who has ever heard the voices of the Oshawa shouting in the day or crying in the night. I pray that if one has heard them calling, they will let me know, as there is an entire mythology of an almost forgotten people waiting to thread its way back into the conscious reality of time.

"Where is our rice?"

It is a simple question. Where is the staple of a forgotten people's diet that sustains them, gives them strength, and ties their people together in a good way? Where are the story tellers and healers? Where is their rice?

Now mind you, I am no fool. I can hear that the sounds echoing across the lakes and through the boreal are the calls of the loon, wolf, cougar, night hawk, owl, and bittern. Yet, it is that I also hear something folded inside of the calls, similar to the songs of whales or spring peepers. Somehow the sound is inside the ear, beneath the sound of the northern wildlife, like voices of ghosts braided into the hollow places within the calls of the wild. It is almost as if the voices of the North Country begin as true and pure wildlife calls, but as they roll across the landscape, they pick up the ghosts of the ancient trees, ice giants, and those of people who have gone before.

I sat down on some reasonably dry moss blankets on the outcrop. Facing north, I was slightly above the canopy of the birch and spruce below. The waxing moon, just past half-ripe, sat low in the northwest and her reflection lay upon the surface of the lake. In North Country, they are blessed with two moons that follow each other about from the east to the west on clear and calm nights. In the heavens, crawls the moon in her sky canoe. On the lakes, her sister paddles in her wake. On cloudy and rainy nights, however, they stay in the lodge and share stories by the fire with their brother the sun, and await friendly weather to race across the lakes once again.

"Where is our rice?"

The Oshawa traders are calling as they pole their round canoes across the still lake. It is surprising how similar their canoes are to the Irish coracles. Yet here in Oshawa country, instead of skin stretched taught over wood, white paper birch bark is sewn tightly over boat frames made of bone, typically elk though sometimes moose.

I never knew if the Oshawa would come to call or to trade, but I would wait patiently, sometimes alert, and sometimes I would drift into the fog of half-sleep. When they would arrive, their appearance depended completely on the fold in the worlds that I was sustaining at the moment. In some worlds, they were nothing; a passing wind, or an owl shadow in pursuit of a wood mouse. In some worlds, they would arrive as bird people, neither human nor bird, yet standing erect. Some were covered in feathers and skins, with wings and bird heads, and wearing breast plates of pounded copper and crowns of woven rushes and cattails. Their eyes would pierce through to my soul. Yet in other worlds, they stood dark and still in the night like the snag of a tree and simply watched and listened remotely.

I invited them to sit with me, sharing mugwort from my ancestors to the east, red cedar for the woodland people to the south, and sage for the desert people in the west. They enjoyed the cedar profusely, and if they liked the sage and mugwort, I do not know. Their stoic politeness would not show me approval or disapproval, simply acknowledgement. I would offer them other gifts that I had brought from other people and worlds, often to their appreciation. We would share songs of our ancestors and of the unseen, weaving them together in a shared song-story in reverence of all creation.

We would trade for many hours - though it is also known by those who are adept at folding worlds, time can be folded as well - so it is hard to truly say how much time would pass. Perhaps none at all. I could not bring their wild rice back to them, at least not yet, but they seemed content to trade stories, song, and lore. With that in mind, I will share one of their stories with you now. Understand that this is a story of an almost forgotten people with their own mythos and way of viewing the worlds that may seem alien to the contemporary reader. Worry not, for our stories make little sense to them as well. Read it like you are washing dishes or chopping firewood, this is not a romanticized tale with a simulated epic finale; it is simply a story of the Oshawa.

ɔΨ⊃

Sugwaundugah sings the ripening songs. There are many who sing the songs of seeding, of harvesting, of drying, and of weaving canes into clothing and mats. Sugwaundugah was the only one who heard the call of the bittern on her long-nights, and so she had moved into the small lodge by the rice breaks in the shallows.

She kept her round boat underneath her house, as that has always been the way of the Oshawa. The house sits on stilts in Sky where all of the Bird People live. Her boat that gathers food sits beneath the house on Water-Earth in order to sustain its flight. If the boat were ever empty of rice and game, then the house could no longer dwell in Sky. Hands and limbs would grow weak. Wings would tire prematurely, and the lake would eat the Oshawa.

The round-boat helped Sugwaundugah remain in this world. Without it, she would sink between the folds of the worlds and be lost, and the songs of ripening would be lost with her. The round-boat kept her afloat in Water-Earth. Her songs were threaded into a bone needle, like finely corded birch bark. As she sang to the rice breaks, she threaded her needle into the world of the sun. As she sang to the sun, she threaded her needle through the house of the rain dancers. As she sang to the rain dancers, she threaded her needle into the house of the earth snakes. As she sang to the earth snakes, she threaded her needle into the bones of her ancestors who had been stitching the world together since the beginning, long before the worlds were made flat by intellect, and made narrow by Time's incipient overthrow of Creation.

With her bone needle, pole, and songs, she gently entered the surfaces of the worlds and stirred them together with just the right ratios.

She was grateful for the singer who lifted the sun from his nest in the forest. If she had to wake the sun every time she entered his home, she imagined it would be much more difficult to convince him to give her some of the threads of heat for her needle. Sugwaundugah was grateful to all the singers. Without their songs, the folds between the worlds would become very difficult to stitch together and the Oshawa would be hungry.

"Where is our rice," they would ask, as they searched for the seams between the worlds to stitch them together in the balanced way of things.

A bittern calls, "rice cakes... rice cakes."

Songs are songs. They bridge the worlds together and sustain an ancient harmony.

Sugwaundugah sings the songs of ripening and stitching. Without her songs, there is no rice.

# Tsal'kalu and the Snake

Long before the Qualla Tract was established, before the *Tsa'lagi* had settled *Kîtu'hwâ*, or even before the *Nûñnĕ'hĭ* and *Yûñwĭ Tsundi'* had built their great townhouses in the highlands, above waterfalls, and on bald mountains where no timber grows, the heart of what we now know as the Southern Appalachian Mountains was sparsely populated by ogres, slant-eyed giants, and tree people. The ogres tended to enjoy caves and boulder fields. The slant-eyed giants, or the *Tsûnil'kâlû*, dwelt on the open balds, high ridges, and granite outcrops where they could enjoy a bit of fine weather (as their eyes helped keep out sun and rain). The tree people mostly kept to the deep coves and rich northwest facing lower slopes of mountains, spending most of their time nurturing the tree groves.

For the most part, these primordial races kept to themselves and to their arts. Little is known of most of them, other than a story here associated with a certain mountain, or a song there, associated with a specific cave or cove. These races were either pushed out of the region entirely, or to remote reaches during the incursions by the *Nûñnĕ'hĭ* and the *Yûñwĭ Tsundi'*. As far as what is known, the *Nûñnĕ'hĭ* formed a loose alliance with the tree people which allowed the latter to tend to massive ocean-like forests of chestnut and beech in *Kîtu'hwâ* and the oaks and pawpaws in *Unaka*. This symbiotic alliance carried over with the *Tsa'lagi* who slowly displaced the *Nûñnĕ'hĭ* and eventually the *Yûñwĭ Tsundi'*. This relationship of land and forest stewardship was almost lost entirely during European colonization. To this day, in remote ancient forests of the highlands and border lands of Santeetlah, the tree people have been observed, if only for a moment, walking amongst the trees, and maintaining the conscious web of the living forest.

Of the ogres, little is known. Some have been seen at play in the gorges and craggy peaks where the spruce is thin and abundant rock

23

tripes soak in intermittent mists. It is believed that the ogress of *Unaka Kanõos* still dwells in her cave, ready to devour any would-be medicine walker. Fresh bones can still be found at the base of her great fortress in the highlands, for there are still those adventure seekers who leave the world of humankind to never return, or whose hunger for power exceeds their capacity to see demons hidden under the glamor of beauty.

Of the giants, the *Tsûnil'kâlû,* little is remembered. There are tales of the giants returning from their new home in the land of the setting sun to visit their ancestral lands and to share feasts with the sons and daughters of the *Tsa'lagi* and the *Yûñwĭ Tsundi'*. It is rumored that they never made amends with the *Nûñnĕ'hĭ* after the War of the Mounds during the Early Woodland period. The *Nûñnĕ'hĭ* custom of clearing land, building ceremonial mounds, and cairns never sat well with the giants. The giants were offended not only by the desecration of their ancestral lands, but also by the fact that the *Nûñnĕ'hĭ* could see them eye-to-eye from the tops of their mounds.

The copper and mica helms and breastplates of the *Nûñnĕ'hĭ* elite, as well as the large open areas cut into the forest, blinded the slanted eyes of the giants and infuriated them beyond any peace talks. The changes to the landscape eventually brought them to war. First, the War of the Sticks, in the valley of what is now known as the Little Tennessee River, and then the War of the Mounds, which encompassed the entire region. The giants were crushed in the War of the Sticks and retreated into the passes of Unaka. And though they were victorious in the War of the Mounds, their losses were so great that they followed the path of the dream canoe to tropical islands in the far west where they still live today and serve in the Lehua groves of Pele and Hi'iaka.

Regardless of the sadness at the loss of the race of giants, there are enough tales still present of giant observations in the Southern Appalachian Mountains to help us recall that in their final decision to move west, one family of dissenters, who had some of the largest stakes in the region, decided to remain behind. It is believed that at least one giant and his brother, and perhaps one of their wives, still cling dearly to the remnants of their domain, forgotten by most, and honored by few, with the exception of a handful of descendants of the *Tsa'lagi*. The *Tsa'lagi* and the *Yûṅwĭ Tsundi'* know him to be the prehistoric king of the giants, and like an honorable captain of a ship, would remain aboard until the end. Tsul'kalu (or Judaculla) is his name.

The *Tsa'lagi* and the *Yûṅwĭ Tsundi'* respected and revered him as the guardian of the wilderness. They paid him tribute, and sought his aid in any hunt, in this world or the Other. Tsul'kalu was the lord of all four-legged and winged creatures, and if he deemed one unworthy of a successful hunt, then a hunter would go home empty handed. Yet, if a hunter played into his favors, the hunter may find enough game to feed his entire village with one bow shot. This is the way of things.

Often, people think of giants as rude or cross, at least belligerent and unrefined. However, the *Tsûnil'kâlû* were quite wise in the ways of the ancient harmonies, of magic and illusion; and, maintained a fabulous oral tradition that would take ten human lifetimes to scribe and collate. Tsul'kalu, his brother Indrâ'kalu, and their wives are the only living guardians of these ancient traditions. They ward the gates in the celestial dome between this world and the Realm of the Blessed, the Enchanted Isles, and the firmament.

The stories that most often blow on the wind in contemporary times, as to the exploits of Tsul'kalu, are of wild parties that see the span of days come and go like the breath. For days and nights they arise, drummers and dancers from all the worlds, here and other, to revel in story, song, feasting, dancing, and merry making. A few human souls have stumbled into his court and verandah on these occasions quite by accident. Some have returned dazed from the radial light of a thousand suns. Others become to deaf to all things except otherworld music that bends the inner ear to hear things unheard. Others never return. They remain to serve this colossal Lord of the Forest in his timeless realm.

25

Be it as it may, in these times when most people walk about blind to the layers folded into this world, few who call the Southern Appalachian Mountains home have ever even heard of Tsul'kalu or his kin. Fewer folk still would seek him out in the wilderness. And fewer folk still will ever see him or attend his court in the thralls of wild celebration. But there are those few, whose bodies have been hardened by the rigorous trekking and mountaineering of the back country, yet whose minds have been softened by reverence, who on a summer's night have heard the drums of Tsal'kalu and his retinue of guests. Perhaps they have even seen the eerie lights of their fires illuminating the top of a mountain just across a valley. The hardened mind, whether from an over indulgence in intellect or the engineered entrapments of concrete and steel, will put it aside with a laugh, or never see or hear them at all. It is a pity that the Earth has been made flat again by intellect.

"Ah-ha, I am hearing the wings of a grouse on an old hollow oak, and the wind blowing through caverns and deep gorges," one might try convince themselves. "And these lights must be some type of static electricity or a storm on the horizon."

Yes, perhaps this is true. But what makes the grouse pound the log in jubilee, and why is the lord of heaven stirring the stars into an electrically charged, ionic play of light? For the softened mind drops into a place of heritage and knowing that runs like rivers of DNA through the marrow of our bones. Perhaps, perhaps the one-folded mind is correct in the initial assessment of the grouse. But the two-folded mind sees that the grouse is animated by a mystery of its own free will that calls to a mate to dance. And the three-fold mind sees that the drumming and the calling is a continuation of the eternal current of creation in full celebration. The four-folded mind sees that dancers and the drum are the beckoning of the Lord of the Forest and all that is of this world and the other to celebrate. The many-folded mind sees that there are layers upon layers of truth that can be fine-combed to delineate the boundaries, or can be celebrated in the infinite glory that we call magic and mystery. Then again, the Earth becomes round, eternal, and full of wonder.

In awe and reverence, the mind rejoices in fullness. The pounding of the grouse upon the hollow oak *is* the drummers of Tsal'kalu. Let us dance the stars through our bodies into the earth that our sweat can nourish those seeds into germination. Let us pour our sweat upon root, stem, leaf, flower, fruit, and seed that we can harvest the abundance of creation to be served at the table of the heart.

In revelation, the softened mind is transported to a great fire, where dancers swimming in starlight and bedecked with the feathers of hawk, eagle, owl, grouse, and countless other birds are rising from the ferns, herbs, trees, and rocks. There Tsal'kalu sits on his throne of granite, moss, and rock cap fern, smiling while all his guests and kin dance madly. He will likely offer his guests a seat, a drink, and perhaps a drum. Perhaps the Prince of the Great Horned Owls will call new guests to dance by the fires. As a guest, one could revel all night, or for a thousand years, and wake in their quiet camp in the morning, or wake in a time beyond time.

The mind that remains soft will smile whenever the memory surfaces. The mind that grows hard with time or the weight of the world will push it aside as illusion or fanciful childhood memories. And who is to say, to a one-folded mind, that they are wrong? Try to calculate the probability of Otherworlds when all of the equations, factors, and variables that are discernible are only of this world. Try putting it in legal writing (though they may ask you to drink heavily before you read it and sign away your ancestors' lands), or sell it on the future's market. But perhaps when the hardened mind becomes soft again at the time of crossing over, they will smile and remember the fires and dancing, and Tsal'kalu.

ɔΨɔ

It is known among the record keepers, that those of the Otherworlds, be they gods or goddesses, star people or telluric dragons, immortals or angels, be they benevolent or malevolent, require a medium here in the one-folded world in order to sway the tides of the multi-fold universe. Most actions and interactions mean little in the grand scheme of things. Geologic time and that which is beyond time, has a way of wiping clean all that has gone before and all that will come. Yet, there are moments in time, like there are key places on earth, that are so monumental and powerful, that effective change focused therein ripples out into the entire universe. It is in these moments and places, which often are one in the same, when that which is greater than time will step through the folds between the worlds and enact change through a medium or emissary.

The emissary may appear as anything. Human history has shown us they the wear the skin of prophets, priests, priestesses, warriors, tyrants, dictators, shamans, philosophers, poets, bards, and so on. Some create bigger ripples in the pond than others, but it matters not. One thing is quite clear, however, that something from outside the one-fold fabric of human reality reaches into this world and touches someone. Whether that Being outside of time gave the human emissary a choice or not, varies from story to story. All that is known is that they were touched and therefore chosen. It may be that all are chosen, but few answer the call, fewer still say "yes", and fewer still say "yes" and have the strength and courage to allow the greater light to fill them and become tangible in this world.

The following story is one of these tales. It is a story of Tsal'kalu reaching through the folds of the worlds, to secure an emissary to speak on his behalf in the circles of human society and time. And so the story begins...

ɔΨᴄ

A'tali'kuli was not a quiet man, nor was he bawdy or brash. Actually, he enjoyed a fine balance of the marketplace environmental, with plenty of hermit time for contemplation. Mostly he enjoyed long walks under the golden green leaves of beech, ash, and basswood in the morning and evening. He was often found wandering by himself in the deep wood, or by the river under sycamores, black willows, and red maples. Yet, too, he was often found dancing in ecstatic wonder in throngs of people at tribal gatherings, or laughing merrily with his arms around a dozen or more smiling folk.

A'tali'kuli had a simple home in the highlands were he kept his garden and tended to the trees and waterfalls daily. It was his joy to seek out the trails of the little people and follow them until they ended at some great tree, a hole in the ground, or a granite cliff.

He would smile knowingly to himself, and say, "Pleased to make your acquaintance," imagining himself invited into some great lodge or otherworldly palace where the people were fairer, the food of superior quality, and the light of day a bit brighter and less intense than the world he walked in.

This is why he enjoyed time to himself, being that others may have found discomfort in all of his chivalry and oddity with unseen folk. Most people would have thought him mad. And really, it was more of a burden to drag anyone along for a long walk as most people did not have the patience to slow down their minds enough to surpass earthly needs, desires and frivolities.

"We are lost," they would complain, "and our stomachs want for more than the fairy food found on rocks, upon bushes, and in the earth that you are feeding us."

So, A'tali'kuli kept most of his adventures to himself and spoke of them to only a few people who perhaps had enough folds in their mind to digest a few kernels of truth from his stories, or to slow down enough to contribute their own.

Tangible or intangible, stories or experiences, whatever the case may be, the other truth was that whenever A'tali'kuli would come down from the highlands to the village fair or the marketplace, his very joy of seeing people was intoxicating and would spread like a wildfire before and after him. It was almost as if the Otherworldly mantle of eternal joy and revelry that he touched in his wanderings would descend down the mountain in an invisible retinue at his back, bringing merriment to all who were drawn under its cloak. An alluring tide would wash over any who did not resist its merry beckoning. It was almost as if their bodies and spirits were animated by something larger than life. And it was contagious. In a matter of moments, a normal every day street fair would turn into a colorful festival filled with laughter, singing, dancing, wrestling, and music.

As this is a story about A'tali'kuli, it is easy to see that he had an effect on the villagers, or perhaps it was the essence of the Otherworld he so loved and respected that emanated from him like a summer breeze. Yet, for all those villagers, all they knew was that they liked him, or at least most of them did.

On rare occasions, A'tali'kuli would invite some of his friends from the village for a walk in the forest or along a river. Occasionally, these walks would fill him with great joy, but most filled him with sadness and longing. He wanted to step off the path upon which they walked. It was designed for humans. He wanted to follow the almost inaudible music of the birds and flowers. His desire to feel the unseen trails beneath his bare feet or in his heart was greater more often than not than his desire to maintain company, no matter how tasteful. He wanted to follow the obscure trails of his mind's eye to some forgotten door or cave, lay down his mind, and bask in the glory of the primordial mysteries. As a bee sees the invisible light extensions of petals as an alluring pathway to the heart of a flower, the mystic sees the invisible way to the nectaries of the Otherworld.

It so happened that on just such a late winter jaunt with friends, the path led them into a deep and ancient wood, long before the sun set on the last day in the Age of the Hemlocks. Buckeye, hemlock, red maple, basswood, and other trees grew to such enormous proportions that it was easy for all to feel as if they were in the Blessed Realm. A'tali'kuli was almost certain that they were in a grove guarded by the ancient tree giants of forgotten ages. He could feel a primordial presence all around them. *Nûňně'hĭ* bones were buried in the Rhododendron-enshrouded mounds along the mountain stream. Like a thoroughbred trapped in its racing gate, their spirits were anxious to ride out on a full moon, when the canopy of the forest swims in silver light.

Every opportunity that A'tali'kuli could seize upon, he would quietly slip away from the main trail to listen, watch, and follow threads of subtle perception of something awaiting discovery or discourse. Yet every time he would just begin to hear the song of the forest and follow a lead on a path, one of his village friends would feel his absence, and chase after him, calling, "Where are you going...can I come, too?"

"No," he would think, "no. I do not believe that you can come to where I would go. With all that shouting, I will not be able to hear the music, and with all of the random chattiness of the mind, we will not be able to find our way."

But he would remember the gold of friendship and would instead say, "Yes, please come. I am going to the stream to look at stones in the bottom of the water, to watch the small fish glide, and use a Christmas fern for a pillow. Together we can watch the sun peek through the boughs of these great trees overhead."

And he would smile and take the hand of his friend and together they would walk in kind, step to the stream, and do just as he said. There was deep magic in those bonds of friendship, for sometimes good company is the best medicine in the entire universe.

As the day wore out, the mists began to form in the tree tops as the sun settled over the ridge. Friends wondered here and there, singing and playing, or sitting and watching the bounty of life that is held in ancient living places. Some drank in the beauty while others play acted it. A'tal'kuli was outwardly filled with joy, but was inwardly depressed as he could feel some other mystery at calling to him. He could sense it beckoning from under the din of laughter, and speaking quietly under the babble of the stream tumbling over stones and logs. There was an invisible unique trail that he never had followed before and could not follow now due to the company that he kept.

Night settled her mantle over the mountains and coves. The band of merry-makers began their reluctant journey home. A'tali'kuli walked slowly, very slowly and found himself near the tail end of the group, with one friend chatting earnestly at his side. He was not sure what was being emitted from his friend's mouth, for all he could think about was that something was there, all around and waiting for him. Yet, he could not see it.

His friend asked, "Are you ok?"

That questions was the key that A'tali'kuli needed to open the door for an exit from the confines of his situation.

"Yes, I am fine," he replied, "but I think that I will hang back and catch up with everyone later."

With that said, his friend smiled, quickening her pace to catch up wit ahead of him. A'tali'kuli stopped and took a deep breath. All of the fog within his mind poured from his nose as he exhaled, and covered the darkened valley in a grey and white mist. For a moment he heard the laughter, singing, and drums of his merry companions, but they sounded as if they were in a cove on the other side of the ridge. Far away indeed, almost as if the sound came through a very tiny hole in the ground, and then the hole closed like lips over a tongue. The sounds of his friends were no more.

The heavy mist settled into every crevice that it could find in the valley. A'tali'kuli did not mind, he beamed with the madness that only one who drinks from the chalice nectar of the Otherworld would know. It is a madness that takes one to physical extremes and remote places. It is a madness that can only be satiated when the mind softens to the drumbeat of the heart and touches the place where that which is without is within, and that which is within is without – dynamic stillness.

He smiled. Half open and half closed, his eyes danced behind his eyelids in the tremors of surrendering to revelation. His jaw began to shiver.

"I am cold," thought he, "but alas my bones and flesh are warm. Yet, it feels as if ice were grating through the marrow of my bones."

He held his arms close to his chest in an attempt to contain some heat, but shivers raced through his body like hungry coyotes in a winter wood. They howled up and down his spine, tore through the forested valley of his belly, and crested the ridge of his mind. There was nowhere to hide, for the bone marrow coyotes had already claimed him. The howling stretched his mind across jagged ice sheets and through bitter winds until he felt as if his soul would splinter into a million frozen raindrops, and be lost forever upon a blizzard-laden mountain bald.

Then it stopped.

His shaking ceased and A'tali'kuli found that he was still quite whole.

"Well," thought he, "at least something interesting has occurred on this day!"

He summoned up the will to tread on and find his way back through the hole between the worlds to catch up with his friends - until he saw the giant frog.

The giant frog rose up from the forest floor from wet seeps - a great darkness inverse to a rising sun. Moss and ferns grew all over the skin of this great one, as soil, roots, and stones strained to find new homeostasis with the frog's emergence. Yet somehow, the frog *was* the soil, roots, and stones. The edges between beast and earth were not definable, as even the grey and black trunks of the ancient beech trees nearby seemed to morph and bend with the shifting of the shadows. Then it opened its eyes. Great yellow orbs, like the harvest moon and her double, split the darkness and cast their luminescent gaze on A'tali'kuli.

A'tali'kuli was rooted in place. Between him and the eyes of this great primordial being, a magnetic stillness electrified the mist and became so palpable that the entire forest matrix realigned out of due respect. The quietness was so complete and perfect that it froze the stars in the sky and weathered mountains while civilizations rose and fell like sandcastles on the shores of time.

The silence was broken with a laugh. It seemed to come from everywhere and nowhere, like an earthquake. The mountain stream rippled with it and the trees quivered as if remembering a lover's embrace, anticipating more. A'tali'kuli found that his mouth was also giving birth to part of the rumbling laughter. It was all around him and within him. And They were all around him, emerging from the quaking and the night. At first, it was as if thousands of birds and rainbow snakes were writhing over one another on the ground. The entire forest surged and pulsed like a warm river. His blood and bone marrow absorbing the fresh energy and heat. Flowers within flowers were blooming, giving birth to pathways of all manner of creatures emerging from silver light and shadows.

Feathers and fur moved past him as if he were only a tree or stone. It was almost as if he was the otherworldly creature that none could see. The retinue of fantastical beings kept growing in number until it was difficult to differentiate the end of one being and the beginning of another. Some looked almost human, though not necessarily in size or stature, while others were part animal and part human.

A buffalo-headed man danced past him, chasing a beautiful woman with the legs and tail of a deer. A white dragon as long as the river of the lowlands near his home country had the head and breasts of the Corn Mother as it breezed around his thighs slowly and sanguinely, enticing him to rise from his stupor and enter fully into the world that unfolded before him.

With rising passion and ecstasy, A'tali'kuli began to sway in the revelry. An orchid pulsed inquisitively before him, while grape tendrils wrapped around his legs and held firm. Of all the fires in the worlds, there is no dance like the awakening to primordial nature. He could feel the hypnotic trance - the rhythm of feet, claw, and hoof, pulsing through the earth, following the time signature of the undulating rainbow serpents, who wrapped snuggly around it all with their fluid embrace.

That was when A'tali'kuli saw It. Near the immense, a great still presence observed him. It watched him from a throne of living chestnut oak, gneiss boulders, and medley of ferns. It was he who is Lord of the Forest, Tsal'kalu, protector of the wild places, and king of a people long forgotten. When their eyes met, the jubilee came to a standstill and settled back down into the forest floor until only the two of them remained, facing eye to eye. The Lord of the Forest, whose eyes in the night, appeared like two great moons hovering in the boughs of the oaks, opened the palm of his right hand to the heavens. In his crown of antlers and branches, a lone male screech owl called into the night.

"Welcome, my friend," Tsal'kalu said. "I have been watching you for some time and have enjoyed waiting for this moment to invite you into my court. Now you are here. Be welcome.

"Long have I felt the wind tangle my hair. It has been long indeed in the measure of the precession of equinoxes, and the rising of the sun in the houses of my star ancestors, that I have walked these blue mountains. They have been my home since long before time learned how to crawl. And I have not had a friend among your race in many a turning of the moon. Most of your kind has forgotten that I and my brother are still here amongst you. And longer still has it been that I have folded thoughts with one of your race. Until now, you have been a ghost, an apprentice, a dreamer, waiting to arise within yourself.

"Come, my friend. See who has gone before you."

He extended his great right hand and gestured to A'tali'kuli and to the north, who turned to what was revealed. Behind him, he saw the ghostly apparition of a person who he did not recognize, yet was somehow familiar, like a dream ally, or spirit of one of his dead. Yet wait, there was more. Behold! An entire line of people stretched infinitely at his back through the dark of the forest whence he had come. His waking sense told him that these beings were a spirit line, or the line of those who had carried the light of Tsal'kalu before.

A'tali'kuli asked, "Are you inviting me to be the head of a dragon, a spirit line that is your heritage?"

Tsal'kalu laughed, opening the palm of his left hand to the stars and gesturing to the south. A'tali'kuli turned from the endless river of souls behind him to face the direction he had been walking. He saw the back of a ghostly woman in front of him. Looking over her left shoulder he could see yet another line of ghosts that continued infinitely in front of him as well.

"At times, little friend, yes, you will be the head of this dragon-serpent. You will have to make choices and decisions that affect the balance of things through all time: the past, the present, the future. At other times, however, you will feel most like the tail of the dragon. You will feel used and thrashed about as a weapon, as protection, or for balance and defense. In these times your strength is needed most. It may hurt and you will feel that you do not have control over your destiny, but hold tight for you will always be guided by your eternal nature. But most of the time, you will feel like you are simply a vertebrae in the back of this timeless serpent, which is my voice, my body in time, my vessel through which I move and help shape the world. This vessel carries the immortal cargo that is the codex of the very landscape within which we live and thrive. You have become an extension of this eternal medium which enables the world of humanity to hear a voice from my domain; to understand my will and design; and, to preserve, protect, and expand my kingdom, the original garden of the earth. My kingdom too wards the gates between this world and the heavens.

"And you, A'tali'kuli, I have chosen you to be one of my voices in one of the worlds. It is neither for you to accept or reject. It simply is your design. Make me proud, and remind me often that I have chosen well."

A'tali'kuli had nothing to say. Inside his heart was a knowing of a deep and ancient truth. Many beings in the world of humanity have become ambassadors for benevolent and divine beings of other worlds. As avatars, they help sustain the balance of the harmonies between the worlds and between conflicting forces. Some bring chaos and some bring peace, but always some greater balancing act is at play or being restored.

A'tali'kuli already knew what this meant, to be a voice, hands, feet, heart, eyes, arms, blood, and warmth of Tsal'kalu. He was to be a voice as he always had, for the wild places, the four-legged people, the feathered ones, the star-draped, the wet-skinned people, and the immobile ones. Yet now, he was lit from within and a great ally had granted his aid for the works that lie ahead.

He sighed, looking down at his feet where moments ago, the entire forest had pulsed and moved. Now it was just a forest again - albeit an ancient one - but just a forest. He looked up. Tsal'kalu was gone as well. The infinite line of people extending through him also had faded into what remained of the evening mists.

As he took a deep breath in, the fog lifted. Above him, Orion was settling down to rest with the sun in the west above Balsam Mountain. In the distance, drums, singing, and laughter invited him to set one foot in front of the other and to follow the inviting sounds of his companions. His bare feet found the trail in the near darkness, and guided him slowly and reverently back to the world of humanity, for there is deep magic in bonds of friendship, for sometimes good company is the best medicine.

# Yunweh Tsundi

A'yun'ini crawled forward under the low hanging rhododendron. He was careful not to place his hands on any loose twigs, for the cracking would give away his position. Fortunately, the gorge containing the waterfall he was ascending was dominated by hemlock and white pine. The forest floor was soft from centuries of fallen leaf needles and it was easy to remain silent. The waterfall to his right covered any sounds of his movement with its consistent roar, but he could not be overly confident that the sound of the waterfall would cover his movement as he crept forward. On this new moon night, he could not often perceive the exact location of his quarry. Sliding over and under rhododendron branches, he slowly made his way up the steep slope.

Then he saw her. She was eating at the base of a granite cliff, looking in his direction as if she expected him to arrive at any moment. He stopped, crouching down low behind an azalea thicket. Her long legs seemed to almost glow of their own accord, poised just so to accent the curve of her back. Her chest was full and almost white under a sky lit only by the raiment of high summer stars. His breath was caught in his throat, while saliva began to build in his mouth. She knew he was there. He could sense it by the way she kept cocking her head and looking in his direction. As she peered into the forest to his right, he could see the white of her throat.

He quietly untied the string around his waist, while never letting his eyes stray from her. Running his hands quietly along his bow, he bent it back slightly to tie the string to the nock. He ran his hands down the other side of the arm and tied the string off to the nock there as well. Silently, he drew a shaft and laid it across his left thumb and notched the end into the string. Drawing the string back halfway to his chest, he stood. They locked eyes. Her ears turned towards him. He drew the arrow back past his right ear, aimed at her heart and released. It stuck her in the breast, and her front legs gave out underneath her instantly before she fell to the forest floor.

He leapt out from behind the flame azalea and scrambled towards her on the loose pine needles. Kneeling at her side, he put his right hand on her chest, and his mouth by her ear.

"Thank you, Little Mother. It has been my honor to follow you for this half-moon; to share your trail; to drink the same water; to sleep under the stars near you; to feel the summer heat, and the late summer thunderstorm pound on my back. Little Mother, whose children are now grown and run with the other does and stags, thank you for the food that you will provide for my family. Thank you for your bones that will make our tools. Thank you for your sinew to make fine bow strings and secure our fishing spears. Thank you for your skin, which will help keep my children warm in the cold months ahead. Thank you, Little Mother."

And on he went, as he drew his churt blade from his satchel. Tying her back legs together, he hung her upside down from a thick chestnut oak branch. First he cut her neck, so that the blood could be drained. He drank almost every drop. He could feel the strength climbing back into his limbs. After several weeks of running, pursuing, stalking, and eating only a few dried items in his satchel, he was famished. He kept speaking to her as he began to cut her open from the stomach down to her heart. This was the way of things, as the Creator had taught the People to prepare deer kill for the long trek home.

Several hours had passed by the time he had everything prepared. A'yun'ini stood to stretch. Looking to the dark night sky, he felt as if he could sleep for hours, but he knew that if he stayed here too long, the smell of fresh blood would draw the panther, wolves, or coyotes. He stooped down for the large bundle he had prepared and hefted it over his back. Reaching for his bow and quiver, he turned to be on his way back down the mountain. Behind him, a silver glow caught his attention. He turned in curiosity and noticed that a trail was lit by the moonlight through the ferns along the base of the cliff. He did not recall a trail being nearby, but it did seem like a good route down the mountain, especially with almost eighty pounds of deer on his back.

He began to follow the trail through the ferns, when clarity seeped through his exhausted mind and body.

"A moonlit path," he thought, "how can there be a moonlit path where there is no path and when there is no moon?"

Immediately, A'yun'ini stopped and looked up to the celestial doom of the night. The full moon was at her zenith, glowing down upon him. He turned and looked back from where he had come. Behind him, the trail emerged from a crevice in the cliff. Inquisitively, he moved quickly back towards the crevice to reorient himself. The trail emerged from the opening almost as if he had walked through the little gap during the hunt.

Trying to walk back through the opening was unsuccessful as the doe on his back was too wide to fit through the small opening. Setting down the partially butchered deer, he tried squeezing through the crevice on his own. Once again, his efforts were to no avail. Chills rippled up his spine as he turned to squeeze back out of the opening. On the far side of the valley a screech owl's haunted voice echoed as if it were emerging from a vast cavern.

Struggling back out of the opening, he hoisted the heavy burden of the deer back up onto his exhausted back and looked at the trail ahead. It seemed to simply follow the base of the moonlit granite cliff. He could not be too far from recognizable terrain, so he decided to follow it for a short duration. The soil and leaf duff was familiar to his deep forest feet, allowing him to move silently with his prize upon his back.

The full moon, however, was more disconcerting than the trail or the inaccessible crevice. He looked up again. There she was, glowing down on the forested valley with granite domes and cliffs on both sides. It seemed to him that the moon was enjoying his confusion; causing the granite of the deep cove walls to glow with a ghostly white sheen.

He looked back down to the trail in time to squeeze between two massive chestnut oak trunks forking from the same root crown. After twisting his way between the two trunks and reorienting himself to the trail in front of him, he was surprised to notice that he was surrounded by tall, solemn warriors painted in white chalk. There they were, in silence, a good head taller than him, holding long spears of ash; and, tomahawks of milky churt and obsidian. None of them said a word. They just looked at him gravely.

He did not feel threatened, though they were armed for combat, and a chill crept up his spine. Not recognizing this tribe of moon-faced people, he respectfully averted his eyes. Without a word being uttered between them, he knew that he was to follow them further along the trail at the base of the cliff. How many warriors there were, A'yun'ini was unsure, though he could see least a dozen walking before him and four walking closely on his heel.

Despite the strangeness of the events, he felt oddly at ease, though highly alert to his surroundings and the lithe movements of the warriors. He paid very close attention to the details of the landscape as they walked, for everything he observed was new to him and he wanted to be sure that he could find his way back.

They crossed over a fallen magnolia, and stopped after they rounded the trunk of a mammoth yellow buckeye. Looking up, he found that they were standing in front of a cavern entrance into the side of a moonlit cliff. The cave stood like a dark gaping maw in the face of the moonlit cliff, as if it were ready to chew him up, devouring him for all eternity.

The silent warrior that was directly in front of A'yun'ini turned to him, pointing first at his chest, and then at the other warriors, "Yunweh T'sundi."

He turned his back to A'yun'ini again as the party began to make its way into the vast entrance and up a winding flight of smoothed, uneven stairs, carved from the living granite.

They climbed the stairs in silence. Along the steps up the pathway, silent warriors, women and men, stood watching out over the deep cove below. All of them were painted white. Many had spirals, circles, and darting lines drawn on them in faint blue, not unlike the dark places of the moon's face. Their eyes seemed to follow him, but their bodies never shifted even slightly from their statuesque postures.

At the top of the stairs, the cave opened into a great hall lit with fires of blue, fires of green, and fires of orange. It was unlike anything he had ever seen before. There were hundreds, if not thousands of moon-faced people, moving in a silent dance around the fires. The walls of the cavern seemed to open up to vista views of the mountains in all directions, while also somehow completely contained within the earth. He could see the valley of the Little Tanasee, the valley of the Chattooga, and more. The granite face of Unaka Kanoos in the north glowed in the full moonlight.

The warriors led him deeper into the cavern, past the strangely colored fires and the silent dancers, to stop in front of an imposing couple. A'yun'ini initially averted his eyes, for the beauty of the moon-faced woman stole his breath away, but slowly he returned her intense gaze, for a quiet depth lie within her that was filled with wisdom and sadness. He then turned to the man, whose regal presence was filled with a tired mirth, behind a proud and perennial bearing. Both the man and the woman were adorned with countless porcupine quills, bears claws, dried mushrooms, and pawpaw seed beads. A pounded copper disc hung around the neck of the man and covered his breast, while a headdress of screech owl feathers cascaded down the long neck of the woman and across her breasts.

The man turned to A'yun'ini and brought his hand to his chest and said, "T'sal kalu."

A'yun'ini replied the favor, placing his own hand on his breast and sharing his name.

The woman pointed at A'yun'ini's deer and frowned. T'sal kalu smiled, shaking his head, and helped A'yun'ini set the deer down.

Several of the moon-faced warriors rushed forward and picked up A'yun'ini's deer before he could move and carried it away from the firelight. He protested, but was held back by strong chalky arms.

Smiling again, T'sal kalu waved to a group of warriors standing near a green fire. They hurried forward, bringing with them another, larger deer tethered to a stout ironwood pole. This deer was a strong buck.

T'sal kalu looked at A'yun'ini. In his mind he heard T'sal kalu tell him, "we are trading this for the doe. She was one of my wife's, and it was not yours to take, though you did offer the proper prayers of gratitude. This doe was of the celestial herds and thus taboo. These sons of mine have brought you this three year-old buck in exchange that your family will benefit from your respectful efforts."

It did not seem A'yun'ini had much of a choice, and besides, the buck would provide more food for his family than the old doe and taste much better. He just was not sure how he would carry the buck home to his family by himself.

But as he was thinking this, two of the warriors came forward with an ironwood pole; about the length of man with his arms outstretched over his head, and lashed the buck to the pole by its feet. They then picked up both ends of the pole and set the buck on their shoulders and stood at quiet attention.

A'yun'ini turned back to T'sal kalu to extend his gratitude when the intoxicating woman walked forward and draped a long, white doe skin over his shoulders. There was no smile. She simply stepped back stoically and looked past where he stood. T'sal kalu reached his right arm forward to grasp wrists with A'yun'ini in the People's fashion. A'yun'ini met him in the grip and they touched foreheads.

44

As a last minute decision, he reached into his satchel and handed T'sal kalu his churt blade. T'sal kalu nodded in recognition of the exchange and turned back to his wife who nodded as well.

The silent warriors escorted A'yun'ini back down through the cavern, down the uneven stairs, back out through the entrance, and along the moonlit trail at the base of the granite cliff. Behind him, the two warriors with the buck followed closely. He turned back just in time to see the leaders of the party pass through the crevice in the granite that he had struggled to get through earlier in the night.

"Odd," he thought as they passed through a small chamber and back out the other side of the mountain in a short moment, "that was not difficult at all."

On the other side of the chamber, the trail ended into the rhododendron thicket and oaks where he had cleaned the doe. The lead warriors turned to go back through the opening, but the two carrying the buck stepped past him and continued on through the black heath. In the dark of the new moon, it was easy to see the silver glow that emanated from their skin as they walked.

They kept a brisk pace. Yet somehow he managed to keep up with them despite the fact that he should have been utterly exhausted from two weeks of hunting. As dawn began to break, he was surprised to notice that they were already in the valley of the Little Tanasee and not far from his village. He was not sure how they had maintained such a pace, but they had made a journey in what would have been normally a two or three day trek in less than a fraction of a night.

Before the sun could break across the ridge behind them in the east, they came to the edge of the forest to the clearing where the village groves of peaches and pawpaws were interspersed amongst plantings of corn, beans, squash, tobacco, and lamb's quarters. The silent ones set the buck down at the edge of the forest. They turned to him. Pointing at the white doe skin, they mimed not to take it off from around his neck. He nodded and they mimed again as if it were of vast importance, then they turned and ran back in the direction from where they had just come.

He watched them until they were out of sight, then he turned back to his village. He picked up the excessively heavy burden of the buck and with great effort, slung the ironwood pole up across the back of his shoulders and continued toward his village.

The village dogs began to bark as he grew closer, announcing his arrival. Some of the other hunters of the village spotted him approaching and gave a shout, trotting out to help. Grateful for their strong arms and praises for such a fine animal, they entered the village in merriment.

His wife and children ran out to meet him and threw their arms around him. Tonight there would be much feasting and storytelling around the fire, perhaps even dancing. His wife's hands ran across the white doe skin around his neck. She looked at him inquisitively. He smiled. In silence, the word is spoken more clearly: all will be told later by the fires.

She sent the children off to gather some water from the stream while they headed for their home. Pulling back the woven rush door, he stepped inside and collapsed on his furs exhausted. She smiled at him, pulling on his waist string a bit, but his eyes rolled back as if to say that that would have to wait until later as well. She giggled and left him to sleep.

And deep sleep it was, for he did not rise until long after the sun had set and the fires were blazing in the village center. He stood and went to wash his face from the pot of water near the cold fire pit in his silent home. Taking the white doe skin from around his neck and placing it on his knee; he stooped over the clay vessel and washed his face and took a long drink. He stiffly stood and walked toward the door. His movements were restrained slightly, as if he had been sleeping on stones for months. He pulled back the woven door mat and stepped outside.

46

The heavy summer night air settled around him in the valley of the Little Tanasee. He looked up to the Bear and her Cub in the night sky. The moon was a small crescent sitting on the ridge behind him to the east. The smell of roasting venison and thick cooking fire smoke wafted across his face and brought his attention back down to the earth and the flowing of the river not far from his lodge. He walked toward the cooking fires to initiate the feast, especially as it was custom for the hunter to give the best choices of meat to the elders and to his wife.

He entered the circle of laughing family and friends and made his way to the slab of hickory that was used to cut the cooked meat apart on. He stiffly knelt down next to his wife and reached to cut off some of the delicious backstraps when she slapped him gently.

"You can wait for A'yun'ini, old man," she said, looking at him crossly.

He laughed at her antics and reached again for the backstraps.

Again she slapped him and said, "I don't know who you are old man, or what you are doing at this fire, but you can wait until A'yun'ini arrives and doles out the feast."

Now he was not so sure she was playing around.

"What are you saying, woman? A'yun'ini sits before you and is ready to share the feast from my hunt from which I returned this morning."

She laughed. "You are foolish, old man. A'yun'ini is still sleeping in our lodge from the long hunt and will be out shortly when I go to wake him."

Now his anger boiled quickly to the surface. He raised his voice, "I am A'yun'ini, woman, for whom you are waiting. I am here to serve the feast now."

She laughed again. "Look, I will go get A'yun'ini. You wait here and I am sure he will happily share this feast with you."

Before he could say anything else, she jumped to her feet and stomping off towards their lodge. He tried to stand to call after her, but his knees were too weak and his back would not straighten. Struggling to stand, he lost his balance, falling to the cool, moist earth. The intensity of the unprotected fall caused him to lose his breath. Closing his eyes to the new pain in his chest that told him he had broken a rib at the very least, he did not even attempt to lift himself from the cool earth. Drool and blood mixed in his mouth threatening to suffocate him. He managed to separate his lips enough to allow the blood and saliva to bubble out and catch his breath. Opening his eyes again, he saw his wife burst out of their home crying and screaming incomprehensibly. She was waiving the white doe skin over her head and running toward the river.

"Hmm," he thought, "that must have fallen off of my knees by the fire pit."

He was tired, and his entire body was in pain and the world was getting blurry. For a moment, he saw the moon-faced woman, wife of T'sal kalu, draping the skin over his shoulders. His eyes focused. His wife was running from the river toward the fire with the doe skin. His head spun and his vision blacked for a moment, clearing enough to see the two moon-faced warriors carrying the buck, urgently gesturing to him not to take the doe skin off of his shoulders.

Again his vision blurred as his wife fell on her knees at his side. She wrapped her arms around him crying, "No! No, no, no...this cannot be!"

And there he was, dancing around a blue fire with others chalky white, in a cavern that was not a cavern, but somehow open to the world. Some of the dancers were painted with blue spirals, circles, and darting lines. They danced madly together and alone around fires of blue, fires of green, and fires of orange. They danced to music rich and full of tears of joy. Swaying in a silence so deep with music, moon drops of early spring were enough to peak his dance into eternal ecstasy.

# Polynesian

# The Theft of Hanalei

Anyone who listens knows that the Menehune still live in Waimea and Wai'ale'ale. It is not advised that you should go looking for faery-holes or pots of gold, as it more likely that the Menehune will simply become angry that you may be stepping on their young guava trees or their ginger plants. Unfortunately, if you are too persistent, you may find yourself thrown from a cliff by a passing gust of wind, or led by erosive thoughts into a high elevation bog - stuck to the hips in muck while insects enjoy the feast served so serendipitously. You should enter their lands with the same respect you would bestow upon your grandmother's home: quietly, with dignity, bearing gifts, and removing your shoes before entering the house. If one is blessed with the kiss of the gods, carries the hero's light on their brow, or wins the love of the elemental stewards - then perhaps a pathway will reveal itself to La Puna, the Summerland of the Menehune.

Many who do not listen know that Hanalei is beautiful. The beautiful lei of flowers and taro fields strung between the breasts that are her mountains can stir the passions of any man or woman. Perhaps a long canoe could traverse her waters and bring a smile to her lips, or a long house be set along her shores to enjoy her flowering and the healing pulse of her waters, though her permission must be sought.

Hanalei is a desired beauty and has been since the beginning. As with many things that are beautiful, certain assumptions are made by observers. For some, beauty is to be shunned in order to avoid a loss of energy or sense of empowerment. For others, beauty is something to be exploited and used for capturing and commanding others. Some people believe they are entitled to the gifts of beauty, and either seek power over beauty in order to subdue it, or utilize the power of beauty to dominate and manipulate. Others avert their eyes and heart, assuming much and would rather not deal with the allure of beauty.

Yet, in respect to Hanalei, not many people would wonder why this dark haired goddess moves amongst us, why she haunts our dreams with her beauty, or what could be offered to her enchanted nature in gratitude for illuminating Kaua'i.

The old ones know. And perhaps even the Tahitian settlers learned something from the Menehune before chasing them in Waimea and Wai'ali'ali. They know something in the way of pleasing a woman, and especially a goddess of the likes of Hanalei. The old ones learned to dance from the Menehune. And the Menehune still dance the abundant rains, waterfalls, and rainbow, as well as the eternal summer across Kaua'i, sending their songs across the seas of Ku to La Puna. They give everything.

Aloha!

## ɔΨϲ

There are many stories of kings, princes, and wealthy merchants who would come courting beautiful Hanalei. Some built great and beautiful homes, or expansive fields of taro, groves of guava, and fields of banana trees simply to win her attentions. She would have none of it. She was content with wearing nothing but the mist and wandering the sharp and jagged heights of her realm. Nothing pleased her more than to feel the rain running down her brown breasts and legs, or to gather the birds amongst her hair and branches. No, she would not come down from her heights for all the wealth a man could summon. Hanalei would not be a pretty bird in a gilded cage that some lord of Kaua'i, or any other isle in the fair sea of Pele's domain, could show her off like an ornament won in battle, or use her for his pleasures. No. The wild Ku, as well as Ka'moho'alii and Kane'kapolei, and even hurricanes were better lovers and never tried to own her. They at least did her the grace of removing the hideous palaces and monoculture fields from her feet that the pathetic lowland nobles and demi-gods built supposedly in her honor.

It came to pass that a very wealthy merchant named Malihini'ko could not be dissuaded. Many before him had come and gone, some leaving only after years of persistent courting. Malihini'ko could not be refused. For one-hundred years, he built palace after palace at Hanalei's feet, only to have them washed away by Ke olo'ewa's rains again and again. Hanalei's continuous denial of his courtship only made Malihini'ko furious and more determined. He wanted her sweetness and beauty for his own. And he hoped that she would bring her fertility and rich waters to his drying sugarcane plantations on the eastern shore of Kaua'i. If she would not come of her own accord, then she simply needed to be coerced into what he wanted. He would have his way.

Malihini'ko went to the *mauna* of a *kahuna* named Kapu to seek her boons. Kapu was a lovely woman to behold, and many said that she was a beautiful as Hanalei. But those that spoke as such were from Po'ipu in the south and had never looked upon the beautiful face, limbs, and breasts of Hanalei. Nor had they seen her garment of mist that rolled seamlessly down her sides and hips. No, they only knew of the stories passed to them from friends and kin in the north.

Kapu was the most powerful *kahuna* in all of the Wailua Valley. It was rumored that she was as old as the gods themselves, yet she remained eternally youthful. None could count her years, but generations came and went. Her bewitching beauty never altered. Some whispered in the shadows of great trees, where they hoped her allies would not overhear them. The whisperers said that she was an illegitimate daughter of a Menehune princess, who had been cast out of the family due to her birth. Some whispered that she was a goddess. Others said she came from a land far to the west where many-headed gods traveled on snakes and rode on the backs of great birds. Others pretended that she did not exist and would pass her by in the jungle or market as if she were a ghost.

Her origins are another story entirely, but Kapu certainly dissuaded none of them.

When Malihini'ko arrived at the great *hale* tree that was her home, he knew that Kapu was jealous of Hanalei, and jealous of all that the illusive Menehune hold dear, due to her excommunication. And whether Kapu was a goddess, immortal, or simply illusive, Malihini'ko was a merchant. He knew how to negotiate a deal. And she could not refuse worldly wealth in conjunction with an opportunity for vengeance. And he would get what he wanted: Hanalei.

He sat outside her door and waited without knocking, as is the respectful custom of a visitor at a *kahuna*'s home. One does not need to knock because they knew that you have been coming for a long time. When Kapu was complete with whatever works that she completed on her own, perhaps stepping between the worlds, perhaps hanging bananas, perhaps singing a *kumu'lipo*, or just finishing a delectable mango and licking the juice off her lips and fingers, she stepped outside to greet Malihini'ko.

Before he could speak, she said, "I know why you are here. The Akua o'ka wa'po have shown me while I sleep. Come inside."

Malihini'ko was only slightly surprised by her directness, but he was definitely distracted by the evocative nature of this sparingly covered woman who led him into her home. As a *mele*, he repeatedly reminded himself that he wanted Hanalei, not this beautiful, immortal kahuna.

"Tonight," she said, "I will take you to the top of Wai'ale'ale and plea our case with Kanaka o ka'mauna, the ancient harmonies of this island that were here long before the Menehune. If we can win their favor, then perhaps they will provide you with a boon to win Hanalei's heart, or at least her body."

Malihini'ko tried to offer his gratitude, but found that he could neither speak nor move. It was as if the heat of her voice had flowed over him like lava, cooled and fixed him in his place.

"Do not bother," said Kapu, "for I neither wish to hear your prattling or blabbering, nor do I care about your paltry desires. I am not doing this to help you. Your desire has simply given me a door through which I can step to call upon my ancestors and the root of Kaua'i to humble Hanalei. She has thwarted the efforts of lovers for too long and does not pay respect to those who have gone before or those who are to come after."

With that said, the whole of the island of Kaua'i seemed to shake like a trembling jellyfish beneath them.

"We must be cautious," she implored as the earthquake settled, "for there are many gods, young and old, who would disagree with me, simply out of their devotion to Hanalei's beauty. But so too, there are many who never won her favor as well, that will come to our aid. And there too are those who see beyond outward beauty, through vanity, to the core nature of the soul. I believe that these seeing-ones will also come to our aid, for the era of Hanalei is coming to a close."

Kapu moved about her home, placing things in a shoulder basket woven from palm fronds. Malihini'ko could not see most of what she packed unless she was right in front of him. He saw only that she packed a small gourd drum and the roots of *awa'awa*, but there must have been more for she gathered many items from around her apothecary.

Outside, the sun was setting and the warm winds pushing up the mountains from the coast to the south. Bamboo, caught in the wake of the evening wind spirits, tapped a-rhythmically against Kapu's windows, and against the impatience of Malihini'ko's racing mind. Questions piled upon questions. Rivers of thought eroded his normally precise and calculated mind. It seemed as if a torrent of rain was pouring over the mountain of his consciousness, and the stream banks could no longer contain the storm's volume of water. Mud filled the rivers. Stream banks collapsed, washing away fields of sugarcane. Boulders tumbled off mountains crushing homes and leaving terribly devastated pathways through the jungle. And still the rains came until there was nothing left to differentiate between the greyness of heaven and earth.

ꙴΨꙅ

Malihini'ko woke to gentle rain tapping at his face. He opened his eyes and sat up.

"Ah," thought he, "the earth is still under me, and the heavens are still holding my head. Yes, and trees still stand, rivers flow where they should, and I can almost see the sun through the clouds."

That is when he heard the singing and rhythmic tapping of a gourd drum.

> *No Puna au,*
> *No hikina a ka la i Ha'eha'e.*
> *Hahua i ke Akua.*

And so on. Kapu was singing a *kanaena'e* to win her allies attention for her night's work.

Malihini'ko looked around and was surprised to find himself sitting in the middle of the *heiau* on top of Wai'ale'ale. His heart jumped. How did he get here? He started to send the command to his muscles to lift himself to standing, but Kapu smiled at him blankly in the midst of her singing fervor. He found that again he could not move. It was as if he was encased in stone; the very lava rock that the Menehune hail from.

From the center of the *heiau* where sacrifices are offered, he felt a burning in his heart in remembrance of Kapu's statement that his personal desire provided a doorway to something she coveted. Just as he thought this; he began to sense a tingling feeling on the top of his head and at the base of his spine. He had the sensation that someone was building a fire both above him as well as below him.

Though he could not move, he found that inside his mind he could walk about freely and see quite clearly. Indeed, there was a fire. Somewhere above the crown of his head, a low-ember fire smoldered. Cast in a ferrous light, which was struggling to push back the infinite sea of darkness, were the undistinguishable features of a circle of otherworldly creatures. Some appeared to have the heads or bodies of birds, beast, fish, whales, and dolphins, while others seemed almost human, but had feathers instead of hair, or scales instead of skin. Many were completely indescribable, as they were so unlike anything he had ever seen or dreamed, as if they were abstract mutations of sound, color, shape, and light existing in several parallel universes simultaneously. The feeling that emanated from the whole of the gathering was that they were discussing his fate. He tried to shout at them, though nothing but rocks and mud poured from his mouth.

A small rainbow snake wound its way around Malihini'ko's body, up his spine from the lower fire to the upper fire. The movement of the snake sounded like a woman singing, but he could not be sure. The snake song wound its way around the upper fire where the council held vigil, and began to stretch the opening between the worlds by circling, circling around the fire. At first, the unusual council seemed upset, but the snake song seemed to charm and soothe their apprehension.

Linking hands, paws, claws, fins, and feet, they mirrored the circle of the fire and the ever growing circumference of the circle held open by the rainbow serpent. When they were all linked in a circle, they jumped from their outer circle, through the serpent and into the fire. Malihini'ko felt as if he had been struck by lightning, as a terrible crushing force burned through his mind and down his spine. He felt as if he were standing naked under Wailua falls, being pounded into sand by the awesome force of the falling water, and unable to move to safety. The power of the water seemed to tear him limb from limb, while inside his bones were melting from the internal heat. He was outwardly torn in every direction and inwardly dismantled. What was left of his mind from the earlier storm was quickly obliterated by a tsunami of darkness.

ꙅΨϲ

When he awoke, he felt as if his head was being pounded between two lava rocks. The backs of his eyes burned and throbbed like magma waiting to erupt violently through the crust of the earth. He found he could lift his hands to his head for comfort and remembered where he was, or at least where he should be. He opened his eyes and found himself lying on the floor of Kapu's house.

"It is done," she said. "While you slept, the *Kanaka o ka mauna*, the ancient ones, came to our aid and fulfilled your desire. Go home and see now that Hanalei runs through your fields, brings sweetness to your roots, and waits to do your pleasures and support an abundant harvest."

Malihini'ko could hardly move, much less offer speech or gratitude. Like a warrior who has been on the beach all night fending off invaders and burning canoes, he stumbled out the door and down the Wailua Valley back toward Kapa'a. As he staggered closer to home, he noticed a new stream flowing through his lands that had never been there before. He frowned, puzzled. He had thought the storms from the night before to be only illusions of the *kahuna*, or figments of his dreamscape.

This realization set his body to shivering. He was not sure what had happened last night and one thing was sure: looking upon the council of the *Kanaka o ka mauna*, whether it was a dream or perceived reality, and the apparent earthquakes, storms, and waterfalls, had somehow changed the course of his mind. Perhaps this new stream was his stream.

As he grew closer to his estate home, his stomach and heart began to turn with the strangulation of deep anxiety. It crept up his throat, grabbing the back of his head and his heart with menacing claws, while raking his belly and chest.

58

"Why do I have all of this," he wondered. "What is the purpose of all this sugarcane. How do I own all this? What is ownership?"

His servants and kinsmen looked at him in wonder as he passed them by.

"I must look amiss," thought he.

He noticed that the stream did run toward his home. His sugarcane fields looked more robust and green than ever before, for the field hands were quickly diverting the water to the thirsty feet of the cane.

"That is wise," he thought.

That is when he heard the shouting.

He painfully and stiffly lumbered toward the commotion, though he felt as if he were carrying lava rocks on his back and around his ankles. He saw that many of his field hands were chasing a beautiful naked woman through the sugarcane along the irrigation ditches freshly made.

He heard Kapu's voice roll around the back of his mind like surf on a sandy beach, over and over again, "It is done."

Despite his soreness, he shucked off the inhibiting sensation of the heavy stones lashed to his body and ran toward the commotion. Kapu's incessant voice was brushed away by the leaves of the cane as he ran.

"Stop!" he shouted with all of his remaining fire within.

All of his men stopped immediately, though reluctantly. The woman ran a little further and fell to her knees, panting heavily and weeping.

"What is going on here," he demanded.

"Well," said one of the older men walking up to catch up with the rest of the workers, "this morning we came to the fields to work and

59

found all of these irrigation ditches dug and filled with cold mountain water. We were overjoyed with your luck, and ours, and began diverting water to the other fields as well. That is when one of the younger men saw her destroying your sugarcane. He began to chase her to try to stop her foolishness, but then he was overcome by his desire for her. Other young men took up the chase as they wanted her as well, for who would not? We older men, myself included, began to try to ensnare her like a wild goat, so we could cover her with something to better abate the lustiness of the young men, for we are too old for such matters to be of importance any longer. As she runs, she knocks over your sugarcane with a passion and madness, yet she never leaves the irrigation ditches."

Malihini'ko turned to the young woman. Her beauty and allure melted his spine and his legs buckled from underneath him. He was overcome by a mad desire to touch her. All of his life force dropped into his groin and his hardened canoe paddle pointed directly at her. Clearly this must be Hanalei herself, in his fields.

He knelt down beside her, and tried looking in her eyes.

"What are you doing in my fields and why are you destroying the sugarcane?" he asked.

"Last night," she said, choking back the tears and finding an anger not unlike that of her sister Pele, "a host of elfin came from the heights of Wai'ale'ale and drilled a hole into the mountain of my right breast.

"I thought nothing of it until I saw that they were draining some of my life force away through the drilled hole and it was flowing to your fields and home. I ran down the waterway to put a stop to whole fiasco. When I arrived at your fields, the elfin had already returned to the *mauna*, and I was somehow trapped here against my will. My blood, my strength, and my beauty are now leaking into your fields, instead of back to my lover Ku in the deep of the sea sky rain.

"Somehow, that witch, Kapu, has stolen me away from myself for your devices and hers. Now many of the plant creatures that are of my valley will wither and die due to the change in the flow of my waters.

"And to what end to we owe this tragedy? It is your own foolish desire to grow rich on sugarcane, to fill your coffers, and to hang me in your bedroom or above your bed in a gilded cage. What now? Will I be brought before the eyes of other men to lust after what you have stolen and perceive as your property now?"

The men of the field gasped and looked at Malihini'ko in amazement. He looked only sad and tired.

"So you have me," she continued. "But little do you know that I cannot leave these irrigation ditches, for this land is not of my body. Slowly you will drain away my beauty and power in every harvest of sugarcane that you export until I am naught but a withered bag of bones, and your bed a dry, senseless place where no man would want to lie or even consider plowing the fields."

Malihini'ko's sadness grew. Her eyes finally met his. Both of their eyes were welling up tears. In the blurry confines of his eyes, the ghosts of the elfin and the night's progression crept into the periphery of his vision. He shivered with the memory of the workings of the night before. How his desire had become something of a mad dream. The kahuna had extracted and used his desire to change things. Now that his desire was gone, all he could feel was a deep sorrow for the plight of Hanalei, standing before him in all of her divine perfection of beauty, anger, and sadness.

"*Kanaka o ka mauna* told me this would help to restore the harmony, as they drilled into my breast," she said through the newly emerging tears, "and they always have been kin to me. I do not understand these actions, why they would allow it, aid in its manifestation, or not seek to protect me as kin."

She melted into a waterfall of tears again.

Malihini'ko took her wet hands lightly and said, "Stand and walk with me, Lady, if you would please. Walk with me for a moment as a man and a woman who are sharing tears. In our empty sadness, let us walk lightly as friends across my domain, for I fear this is the last I shall see of my once proud home."

She looked at him in surprise. She saw the deep sadness that had settled in his heart, as well as the deep truth behind his eyes, and the light of Ku upon his brow. Furrows had eroded into his mind from the night before at the heiau, and these same furrows had ushered in the essence of surrender and humbleness. She took his hand.

The field hands watched them walk away. Malihini'ko and Hanalei walked hand-in-hand in a weighty silence, yet somehow the air seemed to be filled with a shimmering, like the music of a thousand birds singing and gentle water plummeting over polished stone. A visible light, like the sun in the early morning, seemed to grow in the place between them. The men watched in wonder as the sugarcane grew rich and ripe in a matter of a few moments. The watched as the cane seemed to be cut by unseen hands, be stacked, and carried on the winds to storehouses, prepared completely for market.

As the sun set, they went home in awe to find their wives telling of untold financial fortune. Perhaps they would never have to work again, and they could spend their time at home with their families and go to fish at leisure for the evening meal.

A few of the truest and most hardworking men returned to the fields of Malihini'ko the next day, only to find that everything was barren and dry. All signs of a palace, of fields, of the new stream, of any sort of mark of humanity on the landscape were all wiped away. Almost as if they had never existed. Except that it exists in this story, which dissolves in the salty tears of the sea and becomes the food of shellfish.

ꝺΨꞔ

Now of Hanalei, everyone knows that she returned home as beautiful as ever and still sings in her heights and refuses to come down for any offer. Also, those who listen and watch have noticed that it is rare that Ku, Ka'moho'alii, Kane'kapolei, or even hurricanes come to call upon Hanalei anymore. Many assume she has lost her hunger to have her fields plowed, or to have birds and butterflies pollinate her flowers. Yet, some few folks know that she has neither lost her appetite or her joy. And these few believe that Ku'haili'moku has been born again of the old world. That he again walks the heights of Kaua'i with Hanalei, hand in hand, bedecking the land with new life and greenery, and that she never hungers for passion for she shares a nightly feast.

Many who do not listen know that Hanalei is beautiful. The beautiful lei of flowers and taro fields strung between the breasts that are her mountains can stir the passions of any man or woman. Perhaps a long canoe could traverse her waters and bring a smile to her lips, or a long house be set along her shores as to enjoy her flowering and the healing pulse of her waters. She is a desired beauty and has been since the beginning. For those who cannot listen and see, they will be hungry and will remain so until they can set down their pride at the feet of Hanalei. Stoop and knock gently, perhaps she will let you in.

# Itinerant Sailor's Curse

Of the elves and enchantresses, I can hardly speak, for the cat stole my tongue in New Orleans. She took it from me when I fell asleep on a park bench in the French Quarter. Regardless, I can sit here and draw words with a pen in the abstract shape of sounds that my lips and tongue once could craft. I cannot find a way to express my concern to you, other than to be sure not to cross a sorceress in the wrong way, especially if that sorceress be an elf, whether in New Orleans, Salem, or Timbuktu. I will explain later.

Hold tight because this back road that I put my pen to paper upon is rather bumpy, but this is the only time I have left to write. There are no handle bars, seatbelts, fasteners, safety harnesses, or even insurance policies that can help one here in the wilds. It is all based on your mettle and the blessing of the Graces. There are tourniquets for snakebites, crutches for maimed legs, and bandages for minor cuts, burns, bruises and the like, but that is only if one is lucky enough to make it off this wild spell of a ride at all.

I am not sure how I got here, other than a Portuguese merchant ship picked me up near the Cape of Good Hope. I do not have a clue how I ended up at the Cape. Please do not ask. I have no answers other than I slept on that Portuguese ship until I woke up in New Guinea. Other than that, I cannot trace a route from whence I came. It is almost as if I was scooped up from a parallel universe and dropped on this rocky road with no name. Not that naming this or anything else does anything for anyone except force something to stay put for a moment or two. Naming it would be to define it. I will let the quantum physicists argue over whether I am a point in the universe or a wave. That is their debate and the parameters are completely dependent on the one holding the experiment, which already defines the results. I am a wave and a point, but for now I am a wave, and waving my hands across this paper with my quill and ink.

So defining me or my location would be to limit the experience as we would of course have an expected destination, or agenda. And having an agenda is only a few steps shy of possession, empire, and dogma. So let us cast that all aside, as one can never, I repeat never, see an elf or sorceress, dragon or unicorn, giant or nymph, when ones carries the burden of an agenda.

There are no roads or signs to point you along the way. One simply must allow their feet to go where they need to go. I saw a map once. It showed how to get from Grailville to Lothlorien, or Gilgamesh to Krishna, but the map was old. It did not take into account that Count So-in-so had grown a new series of mountains around his fortress in Austria, or that the Giant's Causeway between Ireland and Scotland no longer remained above the tides, or that the Gateway to the Sun no longer reflected the water from Lake Titicaca just right, or that that the Icelanders had built a highway right over their elven capital despite being asked not to.

In other words, the map was completely antiquated and therefore almost completely useless. I did manage to follow it to the Fountain of Youth, but a lot of good that did because I am already 13,260 years old.

On with the tale though, as obviously a tale must have an agenda, otherwise the reader grows bored as it becomes too life like – there are no happy or sad endings, just moments. Also, if we are not careful, dear one, then our tail may be cut off... if the dragon keeps whipping it about like this.

ɔΨc

I met an elf once, who took me to sea on a little Chinese dingy called a junk. Now please, unwind the current accepted meaning of the word, and understand that this craft was completely capable of navigating the Pacific Rim and Indian Ocean. The elf was a trader of fine silks and spices. He offered good pay and plenty of time off when at port, so I had time to wander ashore and seek out gateways between the worlds, or at least places where I could slip away from time for a moment and step into geological and mythological time.

At one point, we had landed at a small port in the Philippines, with the obscure Anglo-French name of Ports of Entry. No telling what the Anglo-French were doing in the Philippines, but that is not my business and I trust they enjoyed themselves tremendously, as many of the local children have blue eyes.

I stepped off the junk as the elf was haggling with a rare spice trader from Malaysia. The spice he was looking for was of no matter to me, so I went in search of adventure. I met a shadowed old gentleman in a tea house who waved me over and happened to speak enough Latin to tell me about a local legend of a wealthy seamstress who lived in the jungle deep in the interior. And it happens that this tale illuminated specifically her interest in storytellers, musicians, and revelers. Allegedly, she would host folk of the craft in exchange for an evening sampling of their skills. Well, I figured I could at the very least, entertain her with stories of my travels with the elf.

After some troubled inquiries as to the direction of her haunt, I was finally under the impression I understood where I needed to go. Did I mention not having an agenda? So here I was, lost in the interior jungle of some random island in the Philippines, wandering around looking for a seamstress an old man in a tea shop had told me about. All of this in hopes that I could chase down an adventure, a decent meal, and a good warm bed. This was one of those moments where I, the one in the adventure, was beginning to regret seeking the adventure out in the first place. I could see the old man still sitting in the tea house in my mind, laughing under his breath and in search of his next foreigner to dupe.

I can describe to you the nature of my frustrations being lost in the jungle, yet if you have never been in that place in your own adventure - where you want to lay down and die, but some instinct to survive and succeed propels you onward - then it is pointless and you are well in need of a true adventure. I was constantly peeling off the sticky layers of a thousand spider webs caught in my hair and face.

My bone marrow was shivering from the cold soaking of water dripping down my back and saturating my clothing from sweat and precipitation. Insects were devouring me like a wedding cake, and insistent, yet invisible demons were trying to wrestle away the control of my mind until I could actually see the demons swinging from my hair, stretching roots across the trail to trip me, or leaping on my back to force my angst ever deeper within.

The demons were constantly convincing me that I was lost, on a fool's errand, or looking in the wrong jungle. Here is the catch though - and why I would not seek to delve into the business of weaving ridiculous webs of personal agony for you - because I have found that when I am lost (and tossed in a salad of mixed green confusion) that is precisely when the door opens and mysteries unveil themselves in their fullest glory.

That is why there are no current maps to the true back country. The weakness of assuredness and the security falsely portrayed on a map is not what is found in front of the true seeker. There is no map that can show one the way to illumination.

"Well, we could create a really complex model on this new Linux computer operating system in order to better determine the current location of our quandary..."

No thank you. Maps are useful, but only as a tool. Actually being on the ground and in the real three dimensional world, versus in the virtual world of abstract concepts such as that hidden within models, language, mantras, mandalas, languages, and what-not is so much different. In real life if you get killed, the game is over.

Anyway, I had found the opening in my wild roving. I had given up. I was completely lost. Specifically, I was pulling my hair out and foaming at the mouth by a waterfall in miserable agony. As it is with the mysteries, when one is lost, one is found. In this case, the door I was looking for found me.

It ends up that on this day the waterfall was the front door of the seamstress's home. Except she is not a seamstress in the way most people would think who own insurance policies, or who know where they work every day, or who want to know the price and schedule for everything in advance. The seamstress was something of a goddess, something of an enchantress, and really neither altogether told. And, I had upset her bathing with my ridiculous crying, moaning, and screaming.

Needless to say, she was completely nude and perfectly gorgeous, even though she found my current display of masculinity quite distasteful. My male component told her what I really thought and she was completely enraged. I tried to apologize and tell her that I had come looking for her, but she grew weary of my frantic apologies and turned me into a stone.

NOTE: *I wrote this from another incarnation prior to the life thus described since I will not be able to write it post-hoc as stones seem to remain stones for a very long time.*

# German-Nordic

# Dragon Kings of Gjallarhorn

A fisherman cast his net into the churning surf near the black, rocky shore. The early morning mists sat heavy upon his elderly shoulders, and instilled an impending tranquility across the fjord at high tide. He watched as the end weights opened the net like a spider web. Yet, unlike the web of the spider in stillness, this web seeks out its prey, stabbing into the cold, frothy sea and wrapping tightly around its quarry, as its master draws tightly upon its strands.

"I will pull ye' from the sea," sings the fisherman, towing on the lead line.

The ocean tore at his feet and legs, breaking on dark, seaweed covered granite. To the north, the small fjord came to an abrupt halt at the base of a sheer, two-thousand foot cliff. In hauled he the net, tight to his chest, with the weight of his catch pressing heavily against the shifting stones beneath the surf. Opening the net ever so slightly, the fisherman sorted through his catch.

"No, you go back, lad. And you, no, not today. Oh, little fish, your flesh-stories are not for me or my table. Back you go. Sorry lass, it seems you ended up in my net, back to the sea with you. And you."

He touched the sides of each fish, just as his father, and his father's father, and all of those who had gone before them. Closing his eyes, he observed the sensations within his body as his hands passed fish after fish back into the sea. There, they promptly scurried from the shallows back to the deep, until only one fish remained in the net. As he reached to pass her back into the sea, the warmth of his ancestral light filled his abdomen and froze him in his release.

"I will be your fish," said she. "I have run with the swiftest of my kind, had many an offspring and lived a full life. I will gladly have my flesh become your flesh. Yet, first, listen to my story."

73

And so she began.

ɔΨϲ

I was once a king, a Dragon King of the Norse, whose ways and mysteries have long been forgotten, like the Druid Kings of Erin, and the Fire Queens of the Valor. I will tell you my story because you are a fisher of stories and will sing my telling to those people who have forgotten their heritage. Sing it, but know that it is not the story of all people, for no such story exists in the languages of humanity. And so we begin.

I was not sure that the massive timbers of my great grandfather's hall could contain so much laughter. Mead was running like fire through the veins of the folk gathered to feast therein. Conversations spilled over the sides of their minds as they gripped the rails and masts of their souls so as not to be thrown overboard by the gale of revelry. I wager that we the warriors were the most lubed of all, for we were celebrating the one-year anniversary of our victory in defense of our thorpe, farms, and great hall.

I, perhaps more sloshed than most, gripped the carved, oak-dragon heads on the arms of my seat for stability, as memory pierced through the sober clutches of time, leaving a mist across the field of my vision to scatter like spider webs and dust by a hungry servant plundering an unused larder.

I could see them again, the longships emerging from the grey blur of sea, sky, and fog, bearing down on our port village tucked in the vale in the depths of the fjord. As time twisted upon itself, the hall melted around me into the mists that settled in from the high fells, mixing with the silvery fingers of the sea fog's breath. And I was alone and not yet king.

The braying of horns from the coast-watch struggled to cut through the fog to alert my father's men to the pending attack. The horns were swallowed by sea and fog, and dragged down into the fjord's dark green depths.

"To arms," cried my father, our king.

The warriors and other men were rushing from their lodges, taking up their iron weapons, pulling on their shields, and donning round helms over braids and unkempt hair locks. From my place of timeless visioning here in the high fells, I observed myself running down to the coast with the others, half naked, yet fully clothed in the wild air of a berserker. There was no time to pull on the skins of bear, wolf, and iron; but, it did not matter, for like wolves and bears, when the dens of my people are under attack, our claws, teeth, sword, spear, and war hammer bite with a ferocity that leaves a trail of blood and bones to make any assailant think twice before considering a subsequent raid.

I tell you, I remember the battle. Every blow I inflicted and every blow I received. I remember the eyes of those who fell under my arm. I remember the smell of blood, urine, and other excrement. I remember the inhumane screams of the vanquished, and the victorious cries of the living. I remember watching the shades of the fallen, mix into the mists, seeking the pathway to Valhalla before an enemy could claim the head of the fallen body. I watched the shades of the fallen who did not make it to Valhalla, attach to the sides of their body, howling silently for eternity for the loss of their birthright. I listened as the wind whistled through my hair and under my helm, the roaring of my pounding heart as my blood surged and carried me further into the defense of our home.

I watched helplessly as my father fell to the blow of the war hammer of Erik, the invading king. Despite my already heightened battle frenzy, I was instantly possessed by demoniacal, berserker frenzy. Furiously devouring the edge of my shield with my teeth, I flung it aside amongst my fallen foes as frothy foam splayed around my mouth and my feet pounded thunder into the earth. Rushing through the crackling fires of lodges and outbuildings, past men in the grips of annihilation, I cut my way through the surge to square with Erik. I saw nothing but him. His eyes, soaring on his personal victory of the defeat of my father, quickly found mine and blurred.

His shade recognized its pending death. We both knew in that moment that his soul would now belong to my kin.

"His head no longer needs a body" I thought, and so I struck.

Despite his foreshadowed death, Erik rose to the occasion with abandon. We parried, but the berserker spirit in me was stronger, and the earth current beneath me surged through my arms with every strike from my sword. Erik could not swing his war hammer around fast enough to counter strike, only enough to ward off my relentless assaults. I was everywhere and nowhere at once; slicing, stabbing, and smashing until he fell into a pool of his own blood, mixing with my father's. His spirit bellowed to the Valkyries for a quick crossing of the Bifröst into the halls of Valhalla, but I was swifter.

"No, I will keep his head for myself and my kin until the Twilight of the Gods," thought I as I detached his head with my sword.

The rest of the battle was hazy to me, and it was told that the berserker spirit that overtook my body felled five more men before the host of Erik receded with the tide.

From my current viewpoint on the high glen, I understood why my memory of what remained of the battle had been such a blur. My soul had stood here upon the mountain in the body of a bear watching the fray below. I did not follow my own body into the battle, for the bear's spirit had displaced my own.

In the body of the bear, I turned from the scene and began padding the spirit path to the burial valley of my ancestors. The standing stones and cairns led me on a circuitous route, braiding together the sacred places in my ancestors' homeland. At times, I moved slowly as cold honey, other times, I flew as a falcon, the landscape becoming my shadow. I was seeing places which I had never seen, or at least which my Father had certainly never revealed. Intuitively I knew that I was crossing the Bifröst - the burning rainbow bridge connecting Midgard to the world of the Valor and the Æsir. The Earth rolled beneath my feet as if I was walking on the sea, yet I was upon the back of a great wyrm whose bioluminescent scales were the forests, mountains, lakes, and moon. The pulsing waves passing through its body urged me onward until I came at last to a bizarre, foggy version of the valley of my ancestors. In the mouth of the valley stood the vastness of Yggdrasill, the great ash tree piercing through the nine worlds. The haunting voice of a völva echoed around the valley and within my inner ear.

> *An ash tree stands,*
> *Yggdrasill her name,*
> *A tall tree, besprinkled with shining loam.*

> *From there come the dews*
> *That drop in the valleys.*
> *It stands forever green over the Well of Fate.*

Entering this world between worlds – a bioluminescent reflection of the valley I knew well – I felt as if throughout my whole life, when I had eaten fish from the sea, I was eating the *idea* of the fish in an emptiness - without life, taste, or a sense of the invisible threads woven through the universe. After entering this world between worlds, I would actually taste the fish and see the life braids which were bound my soul with the soul of the Earth.

I stepped into the mouth of the valley where all was quiet under the drip line of the world tree. The glacier-carved fells and dale spread open before me as I walked towards the head of the valley. I remembered when my father brought me to the valley in Midgard as a boy many times. The stone cairns of our ancestors stand along the ridges of the fells. My father and I would walk up the valley as he told me of our kin, the Dragon Kings who had reigned before our time.

"They call to you" said he. "They call to you when it is time to join them, both in life and in death."

He engraved their images in my mind.

"They had beards of fire and ice, braids of flame, gold, and copper; tall as mountains and strong as the golden tree Glasir. They wait for you to do your deeds, and then welcome you to the table in the Halls of Valhalla."

As I now walked into the valley, I knew that I had arrived here at last to witness my dead. I looked to the fell ridges and saw my ancestors fully armored, standing in silent vigil on the crest of their individual cairns, facing west into the wind, from whence I had come. Long banners drifted upon the westerly wind, streaming from their long spears. Still as statues they stood, proud and stoic as wards of the Valley of Dragon Kings of Gjallarhorn.

In the shadow of Yggdrasill, one of the golden lords was waiting to greet me. He was wrapped in an emerald cloak, pinned by a gold broach of intertwined dragons joined as one over his heart. A wolf skin was draped across the broad expanse of his shoulders. His face was familiar, though it took me a moment to recognize him as my father - perhaps as he appeared when he was crowned King. He embraced me heavily and heartily for a long moment; long enough that when I opened my eyes a heavy dragon fog had settled into the valley, engulfing us slowly in its belly.

My father said nothing.

He simply turned to the recess of the valley at his back, as if to say "Now it is your domain, this fog, this kingship, and the stewardship of this valley," and then he dissipated into the mist like a dream.

I drew a long tendril of the heavy mist into my lungs as a horn sounded from deep within the fog. This valley will be the house of my body until the end of days and the Twilight of the Gods.

Echoes of water on rock within the fog carved landscapes into my mind that did not exist - water falling over granite, and towering spruce trees swaying in a summer storm. The warbled voice of an unseen völva crept silently over my shoulder like a dream.

*The hidden horn of Heimdallr,*
*Hidden under the heaven-bright holy tree,*
*A river I see flow,*
*With foamy fall,*
*From the wager of the Father of the Slain.*
*A mighty stream;*
*Would you know yet more?*

Again, a horn sounded in the distance, cloaked in the depths of the fog. I stepped past my father and surrendered to the mist.

ɔΨc

I cannot tell you how long I wandered through the vast white and grey expanse. I dragged my body through eternal moors, each step becoming heavier along the way. My feet were soaking wet as the bog tried to hold onto my boots and water seeped in through the seams of the leather. I pressed on. The cold and wet found the tiny crevices in my skin and sank into my bones like hungry carrion birds. It felt as if ghosts sucked relentlessly on the marrow of my soul.

I cannot touch it, the time within that time. I was stripped of all individuality and direction. I was given the memories of my ancestors and of the land. At times, I was a boy thrust involuntarily into the heat of the forge - pounded, hammered, smoothed, and shaped into new, old, and mysterious shapes, by powerful and unseen hands.

"Who am I?" I cried.

The unwavering eternity of the fog, was my answer, as again and again I was cast into the forge to be heated and shaped.

I may have fallen asleep standing as I walked, I do not know. I remember becoming conscious enough to see the fog lift slightly. Before me stood a great pillar which was both stone and wood, covered in carved vines, braided knots, and effigies. I could see the bioluminescent wyrm from earlier undulating slightly within the knots.

The mist drifted loosely up the fells behind the pillar and revealed a long, low, and narrow slit in the earth that was disgorging fire and ice. The confluence of the lava flow and the glacier were creating the fog as they vied for position in the valley bottom. The lava flowed past the pillar to the north, from the east to the west. The ice flowed past the pillar to the south and also from the east to the west.

ↄΨϲ

I was suddenly torn from my dream walk. Mead poured down my face and dripped from my beard as laughter exploded around me like thunder on sea cliffs. Hundreds of flushed smiling faces were looking in my direction. I was back in my hall and Loki, had thought it a favor to remind me that I was host of the feast with a sound slap on my back.

ↄΨϲ

This is the story that is contained in my flesh and will soon be remembered in yours.

With that, the shade of the fish slipped back into the sea, leaving her body behind in the hands of the elderly fisherman.

"This is a fine catch and will feed my kin well," thought the fisherman. He gathered his net and the fish, and turned his face into the easterly wind, toward home, a village port tucked in the base of the vale in the depths of the fjord.

# Golden Warrior's Prayer

Call the dragons to safeguard the directions so that I may remove my helm and armor.

I have been wrestling with angels and demons. Again, my mind becomes the battleground between that which seeks to rend, crush and destroy me and with that which seeks to lift, illuminate, and fill me with grace.

A storm is coming, a dark storm that will crush cities and close doors. I am almost ready. I pray that all of those Unseen forces who have guided me through the turns in life may come forward in these next few days and weeks. Guide my decisions for that which is best for me, my family, my tribe, and the future of a deep and rich life guided by the mysteries.

There are many doors opening as the field of battle sways. I can almost touch them. It is like a dream. There are weights on my legs and it seems as if the harder and faster I run into the fray, the further the doors and openings seem to be. I know that - gods willing - in a year from now after I have stepped away from this fray, I will look back at this moment with a smile cracking my lips. Perhaps a better offering to Freyja will be due. For now, I am covered in the ice of the fray and cannot move from the fire.

Perhaps her emblazoned passion is the only flame of hope that burns in my heart, which keeps my heavy legs trotting slowly forward. I know that the Lady moves in my life, sorting amongst that which has been slain to return to her fields in Fólkvangr. I can feel her now, holding me, rocking me.

"Gentle warrior," says she, "this is a mighty battle you wage against forces that were never dreamed in the dawn of time, but stand fast. You are not alone. I go before you always. Come, follow me, and for I will give you rest. Wake in the dream. Open the door and absorb the essence of water falling upon your crown, as door within door within door opens, and the current flows in a thousand forms, in and through you. Be again, rivers flowing."

Grace received, blessed be. Rivers flowing... I had nearly forgotten the feeling of rivers flowing through this body temple with the ice of winter keeping me inside. The Craftsman is shaping me yet again at the forge and anvil. Fire and hammer, I have been worked again by this dragon mountain. The tidings in the creaking of the oaks on the ridge under icy winds, tell my soul that the return of Spring will be the most lavish affair, with multi-dimensional symphony of unfurling blossoms, vine, and leaf inviting colorful hues and rich emotions from the most languid audience.

Oh, She-who-is-three come to my aid. Dear sisters, come visit me and my kin in my song. Bless the forge and anvil of Thor. Come and be with me here as I accept this mantle, for both its boons and its banes. Help me get out of the way of myself. May your realm blossom on the land once again. May abundance flow to catalyze your works into action. May the land continue to brim with life everlasting, bring healing to broken spirits, revelry to the Bright Ones, and peace to all of those who call this sacred land their home.

Come by stone, sword, spear, and shield. Come by fire, ice, wind, and dark earth. Come by bud, flower, leaf, and stem. Guide my actions and deeds in the fray on this day. Help me awaken from this dream, that I can push open that first door, despite my heavy feet, to catalyze the chain reaction of doors within doors within doors, that the river can flow eternally, unobstructed through the temple housed in this body. I welcome you here.

Hail and be welcome. Do not let me fail. I am your warrior, and I often feel alone. Help me to better perceive the Seen and Unseen allies, mortal and immortal, who stand beside me as I wake, as I plough on through the fight, so I will not lie down and give into the ministrations of contentment. So I will not give up. So I will not die within. And when I feel the dream hold me with invisible bars: crushing me, maiming me; embody, dearest sisters, one of your sons or daughters, and lift me up to my feet again. Put the sword hilt back into my hand; put the crescent moon back upon my brow; and, the flame yet again across my skin as to strike the fervor of this ancient blood into an unvanquishable wildness.

I am a river, wild and untamed. With the spring thaw, I will crush down through the bed that you have bid me to lay upon this eve of the battle. I will move boulders and trees. I will set the bees a-buzzing. I will stir the long-grass and make the she-cat's heat scream for the return of Draco in the night sky.

For now, I am ice, under the belt of the Hunter. I wait to wake from this dream and sally forth. My pen is the spear; the bears of Ursa are the doors waiting to rise from winter's rest in tales of manifestation of life's weavings. The field of night is the blank pages that lie ahead of me outside of time.

I implore, dearest Lady-who-is-three, do not let the Dream crush me. I can see my hand, my sword, my shield, and spear, for I am lucid within it. I hear the stones singing my name and the names of the blood rivers that course behind me. Help me stand tall, open the doors, and let the light pour across the fray. You know where I am weak. Come, stand beside me in your thousand forms. Where I am weak, come to my aid and help that which is greater than my limited self to be strong and resilient.

Fire and Hammer teach me wisdom.

Ice and Wind shape me. Break away the weak branches so I can grow in strength.

Help me melt into the Earth, that good fruit and seed may garnish your altar again, bring smiles to the hearts of many, and be the grounds for many a good rub on a warm and full belly.

> With Grace you come,
> With Grace you may go,
> But please stay if you would.
> Share my bed, my roof on this eve.

*Jeremy Schewe*

Hold me in the night
And the tossing of the Dream
Help me wake and throw open the windows and doors,
For the sap is rising.

# The Volcano of House Helzegard

"Crush my bones again, you greedy, hungry bitch," I screamed at the mountain. She had been burying me in ash and lava for what seemed eternity whilst I sat in my home trying to ignore her. But alas, here stands my tree and the tree of my mothers. We have called these lands home for as long as the tales have been told. She burns the land and rakes in the reward of a good smoke to honor her ancestors. I will not wait here any longer, nor be dishonored or be made into a mockery in the northern sagas and songs.

Step outside. There is a lake of shadow: deep and laden with the riddles of ancient and living sages - surrounded by ice-crusted mountains. If you catch the current right, you can ride it to the noon-day sun and drink from the only sunny corner of this cold, purifying water. And drink I will, for on the morrow I climb the craggy summit of Helzegard, earthen-fire mother of the north. It is said that young dragons, wolfskins, and berserkers who seek to infuse themselves with the fury of the Æsir, must climb Helzegard's mountain and give themselves to her pleasures, or be forever stripped of their right to sit in the halls of Walhalla.

I know there are spiders and demons along the way. They invite the foolhardy and ill-advised blindly into their webs with promises of ecstasy. Yet, when these demons and spiders have had their way, they tear off heads, gorging themselves on hearts and conquered flesh, leaving the soul to drift between the worlds until the tides of Ragnarök wipe the fjords clean of driftwood once again.

A smile lights my lips. Let them come. I am a warrior of the Seventh House. I have a lineage of gold that streams back through time since the sundering of the Earth. I am a dragon warrior to the bone; with the iridescent armor of timelessness stretched across this body I call my home here in Midgard. I have shared the sacred drink and baptism in the lake, and my heart is armed with passion and perception deeper than any sea. I drink of self within self within self, sourced from a font of divine origin that nurtures the roots of Yggdrasil.

One foot in front of the other, these mountains too are my bones. Who are these spiders splaying their suggestive entrapments before me? Did I invite them here, or are these beasts from another world, sent to draw me into my doom…to set me as a ghost, and all my ancestors, above the timeless mantle of the gods?

No. They are here to test my mettle. Come little ones; let me eat *your* heads. I will drink your pulped brains for my breakfast. I will make a necklace of your skulls and finger bones to remind me of your magic. I remember you. I have climbed this volcano a hundred times in a hundred lives and I will do it again in the next. My will is the hammer of Thor. My dreams are the thread and needle of Frigg. My eye is the eye of Odin, and I am prepared to lay them down in his stead, for they are white with Loki's fire.

Blazed across the rocky, barren landscape of Helzegard, I see the Queen's sacred rivers of fire, running down the limbs of her vastness. She is full and fertility springs forth around her. The rivers glow in anticipation and the sea sizzles wherever she touches its fine skin. There are none here to aid me in this journey, no allies to lean upon when the footing becomes treacherous. There is only me, naked in the eyes of the world, alone on the side of a mountain belching fire and disgorging liquid stone.

As I reach the mouth of the sacred mountain, I am overwhelmed and intoxicated by the fumes and heat that are emitting therein. I have nothing to appease her, I realize. Nothing that is, except for me. Without more than a moment's hesitation, I throw myself in.

ɔΨɔ

No-thing sleeps here. There are no mazes or complicated riddles in the in-between place. One could wander for hours, days, months, years, millennia.    All thoughts and paths lead to the same destination... reflection of one's duty, one's truth, and the nature of one's character and the ripple it left in the world.

Here I am, as always on the threshold of death, looking into the mirror of my soul. And who is looking back at me, but the trinity of a wild boy, a warrior king, and an alchemist. Their story is my story.

"I will drink to that," roars the king of the hall, followed by a great applause from the court, and a gentle nudge from the queen. "As a matter of fact, let us all drink to that, celebrate and sing!"

In come the revelers, the musicians, the exotic dancers, the dwarves, the elves, and weavers of tales and magic.

ɔΨϲ

A smile cracks my dried lips again. The fire in the heart of the volcano is hot. Rock after molten rock softens my sides, my limbs, and my soul. Sandwiched between the massive hammer of the lava and the anvil of the mountain, I wrestle my way through the pounding and find that I am flexible to Helzegard's demands. And, like my longship upon the dark sea, she bends to meet the slightest undulations of my navigation. I cannot see anything for the vapor is thick. My eyes have been melted by the searing heat, yet I see everything there is to truly see from within.

# Celtic

# The Sheelnagig

"Are you serious?  You want me to go in there?"

The gnome nodded somberly, the whites of his eyes exposed more than they had in the past five weeks of our travel together. Surely this was the wrong place.  There was no fanfare of trumpets, or host of elven guards standing at attention.  There was not even a properly tended trail.  I had been seeking admittance into the halls of Fionbar for almost twelve years.  And here before me, according to my well-fed, overly paid guide, stood the lofty gates themselves.

I looked down at my forearms, shredded and bloodied by briar and wild rose.  My silk robes were all in tatters.  Even my beard was riddled with forest refuse and the workings of untold legions of spiders.  Forlorn, exhausted, and physically taxed, my awareness was cloudy.  No conjured mists from a powerful elven magi-king obscured my path. If anything, I was stripped of all things decent before I had arrived to seek audience with the King of the Fae.  The so-called door before me appeared little more than a moss covered granite glacial erratic nestled on the earth, deep in a beech and hazel forest; a boulder in fact, no more descript than any other in the forest.  Well, perhaps a little different.   I could just make out some carvings along the northern edge.  They almost appeared as ogham scrawling, but not quite.

I stooped forward to touch the carvings, when my guide cleared his throat, "I expect I will be taking what is owed.  A deal is a deal, and it is settled now.  So, if ye don't mind the payment as agreed, I'd be liking to make me way home back to the miss."

Right, I thought.  He fears this place and wants to move on, or he has swindled me in a most outstanding fashion and seeks to make his escape.  Yet, I could smell the fear on him like a rutting bull smells it from fifty meters away on a drifter who wakes to find he is in an occupied paddock.

Well, so be it. Pay the wee man his wages and let him be on his way, thought I.

After he was paid in due and on his way, I turned my attention back to the theoretical gateway.

Hmmmmm.......a puzzle it seemed.

Tracing my finger through the moist moss, it almost felt as if the boulder was warm. Deeper into the moss my finger probed, for it seemed there was an opening of sorts, yet I could not see it. The moss enveloped my hand and the boulder shuddered.

I parted the moss and found that the stone was truly more than it seemed. Layers of stone overlapped and met in flowing folds, and I could slowly explore deeper if I was ever so gentle. If I moved too fast, the stone would grow hard and refuse my explorations, but if I moved slowly, the stone became soft and pliable, drawing me deeper in.

I sank my nose into the moss and took in a deep breath. There is nothing in the world like the fresh aroma of the pure green oxygen hiding amongst the twining of moist moss. Opening my mouth, I gave back my spent breath that the moss could flourish. I moved my nose and mouth from one new moist spot to another, breathing in this gift while I explored the deepening cleft within the stone itself.

As I exchanged my breath with the moss on the outside, more and more of my body was being drawn slowly into the crevice until I was inside, completely, the moss closing around my head. The stone enveloping me trembled. And though my eyes could not see, I could discern the shapes, variations, and undulations of this world I was being drawn into.

Deeper I went. Deeper until I could hardly breathe, being squeezed between two walls that rarely host visitors.

Deeper went I, until I my course was uncontrollable in any direction other than advancing. Deeper went I, until discerning the boundaries between myself and the undulating and endless cavern was no longer possible.

Deeper went I, until I could go no further. There were no more layers of soft and warm stone to push gently aside, and yet I had the sense not only of an infinitesimal depth beyond, but as if I were being keenly observed and watched.

I heard piercing laughter crack open the layers behind me; stone grinding on stone. The earth was shaking with laughter and a moan heard within my inner ear, sent ripples and quivers up and down my spine. I was pressed against still softer surfaces and my feet found a warm river pouring over them in the darkness as I was pulled into oblivion.

# The Cave of the Morrigu

The Morrigu is the goddess who wards Connacht in the northwest of Ireland. Her essence travels through iron and she has a potent magnetic allure that drives anything warm-blooded to rut. She wields a strong arm in battle and is emboldened with passion in love. She bares the sword of Nuada in the right hand, and the shield of Erin on the left. In the caves that belong to the Morrigu, her lobelia flowers constantly overflow with pure water, even in the depths of winter.

When she rides to battle with her legions of the Fae, trees bend beneath the howling of her winds and the deluge of her rains. And when she makes love, the mountains tremble in her ecstasy. She is the queen of Samhain, the summers end, and is one of the guardians of the great wheel of the seasons and all of Ireland. In her country, there are many portals to the otherworld in the form of cairns, natural caves, and dolmens. All of these are doors to the Summerlands, the Blessed Realm, the Land of Eternal Youth: Tir na nOg.

She calls to her lover, "Come to me, warrior. Come to me and ride the rhythms of the mountains, buried beneath elf clouds and dragon fog. Tremble and shake. Sing your pleasures as you slide up this falling water that is only mine to share with you from my freedom to choose you on this night."

"Then I shall mount your steed, my Lady," says he. "And I will gladly ride until the sun has risen in the east, and then sets in the west, and your rivers run strong with my seed and yours, bringing fertility to the plains below. Ride and sing!"

The mountains shake with pleasures that only a goddess can know. It is as if the mountain might collapse in on itself, but her lover knows that she has done this before. Whether when she rides to battle, to love, or to rule with a strong arm, welcoming breast, and open heart, the Morrigu will always be found where passion pounds like the ocean against the sea cliffs in the lands of Erin.

*Jeremy Schewe*

### ꝋΨꞔ

A Bird calls from her window looking west.

The lone charioteer smiles as he rides to the stables beyond the sea.

The grass on the mount is wet from an afternoon shower.

It is here that his golden limbs reach into her chamber...

Trembling in anticipation of his lover's kiss.


He has harrowed the fields of the Bird before,

But she teases him into fervor.


Which room am I in?

Am I the Black Raven,

    the Wildgoose,

        or the Wren on this eve?

Which river have I bathed in tonight?


Catch me. Catch me.

    I am gone.


I am neither night nor day,

Gooseberry or Elder...

Catch me. Catch me.

## Ports of Entry

I am gone.


Take me in strong arms.

Bend my bow and stretch the strand taught.

I cannot release the music of wonder

If you do not hold me just so.


Yes, responds the charioteer,

And I cannot fire arrows, sweet, sweet Bird

If I cannot find the key to the arsenal of your heart.

Shall I plunge arrows blindly into the darkness...

Or will you provide me with a doorway,

   A light,

Where my eyes can worship you,

My hands can stir you,

And my arms can bend you to the ancient music

Pulsing through our veins?


The Bird laughs and throws open her chamber.


Come then. Catch me.

Bend me, but do not break me.

If we are to make music,

My strings must be strummed lightly...

Though I beseech you,

Play the drum of my heart with vigor and abandon,

    As if this were the last sunrise and sunset.


How many suns set on that long night in Summer Country?

How many lives of humans, come and gone like the waves on a rocky shore?

How many cities fallen to the hammer of time...

While the charioteer

    And the Bird

Made music on the mountain.


Step out.


Go there, I beseech you.

Go there to the place

    where the moss enshrouded cliffs

        are riddled with the pleasures of a goddess...

Waiting to invite the setting sun to her pleasures.

You may find that the Bird and the Charioteer are still making

        fine music

    Music that can shake mountains.

## Ports of Entry

Music to stir the loins for lost loves and newly gained
passions.


Go there...

But only if you intend to listen

Or to become -

To become a fragment

of the oldest composition of music in the universe.


Go there...

But only when you are ready to surrender

to the majesty of this ancient harmony.


And so is the story of the beloved ones.


I stand naked before you.


I am wild.

I am free.

And so are you.


Catch me. Catch me if you can.

For I may catch you when you start your joyous run....

Catch you and

>   drag you off laughing to the Summer Country

>   For an eternal afternoon

>   Making music with the Fae.


Step up, for the bard, Oisín would speak.


I am a dragon,

Born of the Rainbow,

>   Ward of the Bridge

>   Carried here on Birdsong.

I have been here a thousand upon a thousand times.

Where once I stood in the hall of kings,

I now walk alone over windy moors

>   Or I revel in banshiedhe song at the hearths of

>>   forgotten homes

And laugh under the belt of Orion

>   On cold winter nights

With the Fianna all around me.


I spin and weave under Pegasus and Draco,

>   Summer songs that give the Fae a causeway

>   Between the worlds, despite the pulse of the tide.

I wake sleepers and trees

Singing to them to rise from the deep.

Dord Fiann has been sounded

  For the Seven Winds.

Friends, it is time to sally forth.


Walk onward upon eternal roots.

The trees stand tall across countless worlds.

Dragon song opens doors and windows

That the Light of Erin can illuminate the pathway of travelers...of dreamers.


See the song unfolding before us

  At times in rote

    At times a river

  But most often a road....

   Between the stars

  Between the standing stones

Between the kingdoms of the heart...

Between heaven and earth.


Step down to the circle of stones....

The dragon is the heartbeat,

                lifeblood pulsing -

    Drum calling all to dance

To throw down all walls in jubilee.


Come! The fire is hot!

The Labyrinth's walls are self-created or adapted.

Riddles are only there by our own creations

    Or the creation of others if you give them the reigns.

No! Grab the reigns and ride!

This is your dragon!


Step up from circles of stone

Look to where Oisín sings upon the back of his grey steed...


I live in the Summer Country,

    This dragon am I.

Unveil your dragon,

    This eternal nature are we.

This tapestry of words would be naught without

    the temple you hold in the sanctuary of your heart.

*Ports of Entry*

Drink shall we from the sacred well of our eternal friendship.


Drink. The water is good.

    Drink....

Take the Big Dipper in Summer,

        and the cache at Orion's belt in Winter.

Whether we meet at this crossroads of words

    For pleasure or for tea,

        Comfort or tears,

This is all we have

    Here now

Beyond time, what lies before, behind, within us...


Let us embrace this moment upon the altar of our souls,

    For this moment in how we celebrate eternity.

If we do not like what we see,

    Let us have a charrette and design anew.


And I ask you,

    Friend,

        Lover...

Will you remind me that when I have fallen apart,

T'is only because I asked for it so that I could design anew?

Remind me that I was holding onto too much.

And like a human-made lake or pond

   Made to secure water for the future,

My dams were bound to fail

   To let the waters rush free and true to course

   To dash against rock, stone, root, and sand!


Remind me that I am whole.

Remind me that holding onto life only strangles it.

Help me let it all go...


   Let me cry.


Hold me with love

Until I am strong again

That I can stand at the Bridge between the Lord and Lady and say,

   Yes! I am your warrior.

      I strike with hammer, sword, spear, and arrow.

         I strike true!

   Yes! I am your bard.

      I nurture with chalice, spring, well, and cauldron.

         I fly true!

And my friend, my beloved One...

    I shall do the same for you.


Lord and Lady, guide my breathe,

    My words, actions, and deeds.

And together we will make lovely music.


I am a dragon,

Born of the Rainbow,

    Ward of the Bridge

    Carried here on Birdsong.

I have been here a thousand upon a thousand times..

Where once I stood in the hall of kings,

I now walk alone over windy moors

    Or I revel in banshiedhe song at the hearths of forgotten

        houses

And laugh under the belt of Orion

    On cold winter nights with the Fianna all around me.

# The Fall of Daingean Ui Bhigh Castle

I can hear their laughter and braggart tales - roaring over the din of music, feasting, braying dogs, and squealing scullery maids. It is this very laughter and ruckus that seeks to cover over a deeper fear, or to push back a looming shadow to the corners for the hunting dogs to chew on. A current of darkness lies thick within the hearts and minds of all those who feast here on this eve of Midsummer. I can smell and taste it in the air under all of the revelry, as if the laughter was a perfume masking over urine and filthy sweat.

There is a tangible and formidable power here at Daingean Ui Bhigh. Not ancient like the Neolithic dragon paths of standing stones, dolmens, and cairns here in Ireland, but a twisted primordial power that stems from the strangulation of the natural rhythms of the land by a moldering, conquering people; a people who have left a footprint where they should not have. Daingean Ui Bhigh was a massive keep in the north of Munster, and the remains of the hall that I now sit in could have feasted anywhere between two to three-hundred people.

I smell the smoke, where now great trees stand. I can taste the mead where now my mind wanders across the failing architecture of a forgotten human realm, buried in oak, ash, beech, and ivy. Here, where once Christian men ruled, now has been reclaimed by the Fae. Stone walls erected with order and plans, are now slowly torn apart and reduced into piles of rubble by roots of trees and vines. The trees and their keepers have returned from the archives of time, to seal the gate, and reclaim what has always been theirs: stone, earth and heaven. This is the story of their reclamation of the land, and the return of the primordial wood, as told through the last journal entries of the Lord of the Keep, whose wife still roams the empty halls and winding stairs crying into the night morning for her lover. Ask anyone who lives near the wood. They know she is still there.

ɔΨɔ

We have barred the gate and a great fire is lit in the castle yard to heat the pitch to a boil.  The men are at the walls of the outer keep, in the inner keep, and in the north turret.

Look to your standards, lads.  The trees are at the gates throwing stone missiles in a rain of death and destruction upon our men-at-arms.  The women and children are stricken with fear in the hall of the inner tower house.  Come then bracken and vine, tearing into the mortar, gripping the very foundations of the outer walls, and tearing it apart, piece by piece.

Axe and spear, sword and flame, fly true!  The defense is held as the men-at-arms repel the initial onslaught, clearing limbs, branches, boughs, and tendrils as fast as they come.  Ah, good iron and fire is a bar to anything this feral army of the forest can muster.  Whoa to you, tide of the old world, for this is the time of man.  Stand ye back, wildwoods and wilding things, for ye are no match for cold iron, hungry fire, and the insurmountable spirit of men.

Wait, the eastern wall of the outer keep has been breached.  A regiment of oak and beech has launched an all-out assault with missiles of stone and dried clay.  Under the cover of these missiles, several sorties of ivy crept to the base of the wall unnoticed, despite heavy losses from friendly fire, where they gathered in force, burrowing deep tendrils into the cracks of the outer wall, and have now sapped the wall.  The men are fighting valiantly, but the missiles from the oak and beech units are now inflicting extensive casualties among our outer defenders.  O'Sullivan, captain of the eastern wall has fallen under the crushing sweep of an oak, and the wall is collapsing.

Quickly! Fill the breech!

Men held in reserve are called from the Great Hall, but it is far too late.  The distraction of the east wall was adequate enough that a contingent of elder and ash were able to clamber over the south wall and onto the roof of the great hall. Stamping, stamping, crushing the roof with a thousand little root-feet, the elder and ash are trying to get into the hall from above.

Call the reserves back, for we are routed. We must protect the Great Hall, for our horses have been sheltered there to protect them from the attackers' missiles. Blood and sap cover the walls and yard.

While we were focusing on the Great Hall and the east wall, an oak giant marched to the south wall under cover from hazelnut fire in the west, and ripped a massive hole in the wall just west of the Hall. The hole was quickly captured by ferns and orchids, as they rushed to cover the entry and maintain the breech. Elder and ash crushed through the roof of the hall, while the massive oak beams that once supported the roof, collapsed. The flames quickly spread across the hall from the hearth, engulfing men, screaming horses, and trees alike.

The east wall has fallen as well. Legions of ivy have torn the walls down to rubble. Oak, beech, alder, hazel, larch, and willow are storming through the gap, followed by a heavily armored division of thorn, elder, and ivy. The men on the north wall are attempting to flee the wall to retreat to the inner keep. Another division of hazel thrust their way through the gap and tear into the retreating men with a savagery that has not been seen since the Vikings. The men are being cut to pieces. They have lost all discipline and battle formation and are caught up in the chaos of a free-for-all mêlée.

Left and right, swords and axes swing true, as the men fell trees before the keep. But hold! A cohort of sycamores have cut the retreat in two and now the heavily armored division of oak that first burst through the breech is joining in the fray. Metal is crushed under a sea of wood, leaves and roots.

Pour the boiling oil! Clear the field so the remaining men can find sanctuary in the keep.

Boiling oil is spilled by the men in the inner keep. A coal from a controlled fire on the roof of the keep sets the oil saturated forest of beech, oak, sycamore, and ivy ablaze. But it is too late, for none of the men from the east wall survived the onslaught.

The fire from the oil is amplified by the blazing great hall. When the fires meet on the field of battle, everything is ravished by the hungry flames. Oh, the sight - to see a thousand trees burning and quivering in their death throes. From the east to the south, there is so much flame and smoke that nothing can be seen for the time being. Our lungs are constricting and our eyes watering.

Turn to the north, where maple and ash divisions have succeeded in tearing through the outer keep's gate and have renewed the decimation of any man left in the outer yard. The inner keep is closed to all entrants by the uncontrolled fire, be they man or forest. From the battlements atop the inner keep, flaming arrows are raining down on the renewed assault of the forest. A quick glance to the west brings news that there are men trapped in the turret. They fight on. Spear, axe, and sword are cleaving tree tops from the apex of the turret, while fire and arrows from the inner keep fly true, holding the attackers somewhat at bay. It seems the growth forward of the forest army is temporarily stalled.

The divisions of sycamore and ash that broke through the north gate have fallen. Yet, the men inside the turret are still trapped for now in yet another wave of the forest's assault. This wave is led by lightly armored thorn and bracken. Quick in movement and precise in the delivery of their attack, they are held at bay by the men in the turret for only so long, for the men are greatly outnumbered and grow weary. Support from the inner keep is now all but impossible as heavily armored beech, oak, and ash begin to pound against our walls under the protection of heavy missile fire from hazel and yew. The remaining men in the turret are left to their own demise and will suffer their own fate.

Horns sound from across the river. The Duncan's have ridden to our aid and are riding hard across the stone bridge, bearing down on the willow reserves to the west waiting as defense for the hazel and yew artillery.

Ride! Ride and let your iron swing true old friend! Ride and come to our aid in this forsaken hour, for all is lost otherwise.

But what is this I see as they ride across the long stone bridge over the river? Where is the water? Stop!

A mixed regiment of alder, birch, and willow have held the river back with their roots and now release it in a flash flood that bears down on the Duncan's and the bridge. Turn back, cries the Duncan, as he sounds the retreat. Turn back, cries the castellan, as he waves the standard. But it is too late. The sweeping torrent of water crushes into the bridge thereby crushing the Duncan's charge and our hope of aid beneath mud and water.

To the north, the turret and all of her men have been broken by ivy, thorn, elder, and ash. The inner keep seems to be the only refuge now in a sea of smoke and trees. The walls are too high to climb, too tightly knit to rend, and flame and arrow pour from the walls. Any of the besiegers who would venture to parley, would become yet more fuel for the fires that rage around the inner keep. And so the mantle of Aengus, keeper of dreams, sets upon the keep as night follows on the heels the battle. The outer keep has been lost, and the flames of the ebbing battle rage into the night, filling all of our eyes with the thick smoke of green, living wood.

Many of my men are broken, wounded and torn. Many more yet terrified as to what they have seen on this day. The bombardment of stones upon the keep by the artillery units of the forest continue through the night and are enough to string one's mind out so thin as to break into the chaos of madness at any moment. And some minds it did take. One of the men who had escaped from the fall of the outer keep, threw himself to his death from the battlement into the ghostly flames of the yard below.

The bombardment continues through the night and is slowly dismantling the battlements on top of the keep, but it does not seem to be impacting the structure of the keep proper. A regiment of oaks, ivy, and reckless elder and thorn camp the night away on the south side of the keep within range of our fires, but we have abated our own defensive assaults somewhat in order to reserve missile material for the pending assault at dawn.

Even more disconcerting, a heavily armored company of beech and oak are huddled closely to the southern wall, where the fires have died back. What they are doing, it is hard to say, for the other sides of the keep are free and remain on an edgy standstill, beneath a barrage of missiles from the artillery units in the dark.

I am going to sleep for a bit if I can, under the din of this battle and tension. We will all need our strength to struggle yet another day to hold back the tide of the forest from taking over our keep.

ɔΨϲ

I wake from troubled sleep to find the south side of the castle in pitched battle. We have suffered few casualties overnight, but the numbers of fallen trees are innumerable. The inner keep remains in good standing with smoldering trees scattered across the yard as I left it when I slept for those scant hours in the night. Steadfast beech and oak, though many have been burned to charcoal stumps, hold their ground against the south wall, while division after division of trees and vines throw themselves at the walls around them.

Suddenly, the attack takes on a whole new level of ferocity. A cold winds pours down on us from the north, which brings a temporary relief to those of us in the hot tower, but then brings a chill to the spine as again we are assaulted from all sides just as the sun peaks over the eastern horizon behind the billowing smoke of the inner keep. They are coming from all sides now. All to arms! To arms!

One of the battlements has been crushed with a dozen men inside. Unleash oil and fire and all the reserves. Bring down this mad forest army!

Looking to the west, a battery of missile-projecting willows has gone up in flame from some of the spilled oil, rolling downhill, and across the lake. A site to behold and it lifts the hearts of the men who counter-attack with a new vigor. Oh, how the boughs and leaves sputter and pop, throwing flames 20 meters in the air. Stay out of the world of men!

The assault on the south wall has increased in ferocity. The trees are throwing thorn and vine up onto the battlements to combat with us in hand to branch combat. They are tearing us apart from the top down or inside out. To the ramparts with iron, lads! Clear the bracken before they take hold and rip us asunder.

The fray is all over us now. We are running low on arrows and oil. Keep the oil and arrows on the hottest areas, so we can sweep the yard with fire when necessary. I am not sure how much longer I can write, I must take up my father's sword and shield and join the pitch. I fear we may lose the keep before noon. There will be no survivors in this battle, for we have made an enemy out of the forests, the protectors of this land.

I pray for myself, my family, and the souls within which I vowed many years ago to protect. May we find our glory resting in Heaven when we leave this wicked Earth.

What is that? My God! The south wall of the keep is collapsing. The heavily armored oak and beech have been digging their roots in all night to sap us. They are in the keep! They are in the keep!

ɔΨϲ

A heavy mist has settled around the Great Hall. Last night in the pouring rain and howling winds, I could hear the Lady wailing for her loss. It is her wailing that calls to the ancient ones to return here from the Otherworld to what was once their own. And so we return on the backs of great birds and sea monsters. Meanwhile, we can listen as the raindrops speak on behalf of the forest.

Tapping, tapping...and dripping, dripping upon soft earth, we call. Where once mud, feces, animal piss, and hewn stone obstructed our landing upon the earth, now ash, oak, beech, yew, elder, thorn, willow, alder, fern, and ivy embrace us and drink deep. They catch us. Like music, we light our feet upon their blossoms in spring, leaves in summer, and buds in the winter. We slide into living soil where we are again the song of the earth, seeping into mycorrhizae and root hairs, as we come together again in kinship in sap, streams, lakes, rivers, and sea. Where once, drunken, fool hardy, and power-hungry creatures decimated the beauty of creation, we thrive again.

Ancient forests stood here once. They were filled with the voices of wild creatures, and the love play of gods. These were felled by axe, sword, and fire to push back the indigenous voice of the land and replace it with a civilized stamp of approval from another land far to the east. Now here stands a young forest, whose limbs reach again from the earth to the heavens. Yet, this cathedral is an empty forest. It waits for the silent foot falls of the Fae. It waits for the return of the voices of the wilding creatures. It waits for the gods to awaken again in their love play.

# Oweynagat na Rath Cruachan

---

Aye, this one follows a bit more of a theatrical thread in respect to the Celtic holiday of Samhain as an Irish tradition. Some edits and additions by Alexander Tait.

Casting:

Hero (Fionn mac Cumhaill)

8 Wards of the Wheel

Morrigu

Brigid

Holly King/Grey King

Mirror

The Fae

Wildman & Wildwoman

**SCENE:** *The sun has set. An evening mist lies heavy on the canopy of a forest covered mountain. A dragon cloud passes silently over a stand of ancient oaks and hickories, while a quiet symphony of the Danu is caressing the landscape, calling the mist to dance on mosses and frost-bitten leaves. Within the ancient grove of oaks and hickories, under the guise of Rath Cruachan, a deep cave, known to the Children of Erin as Oweynagat, that is often cold and moist, is ringing with the voice of the Morrigu, and glowing with the heat of her fire. From that which is dark and cold, yet light and warm, comes the mad laughter of She who Makes and Destroys.*

*[The hero is high on the balcony. Begins to climb/rappel down a rope from the balcony and narrowly approaching Rath Cruachan,*

*sidhe of the Morrigu. The Morrigu is within her cave, Oweynagat, under the mound, preparing her Samhain fire.*]

**Morrigu:** [*high energy, cackling and angry*] Get out! Get out! There is no room for you here in the dark vastness of my cavernous hold, Rath Cruachan. On this night, the Cave of the Cats, doorway to the Summerland, is mine! What is this about? Slithering and sneaking into my sacred chamber on a night such as this? Did you hope to have your way with me, fool? Do you suppose I would crown you King of the lands of the Fae? How many lies do you think you can tell yourself before the ravens come to feast upon your soul?

This is my Womb! I choose who is to die and who is to be reborn. With a flick of my hand, my wolves would have you, my crows descend upon you... dismembering you from the inside out. There is nothing you can hide from me! In this Dream, you are nothing but bones and ash. I see your power games, your pulling on the strings of others hearts...wanting them to yearn for you and for you alone, as if you were a god or goddess.

[*enter the two mirror holders with mirror...the hero can no longer see her, he sees her only as a reflection through the mirror*]

Do not think you can manipulate your way into the Summerland with pretty words, flowery speech, and saintly adornment. Have you earned any of it?

Or have you bought it all from the peddler in the village so that your friends will smile and say, "oh, yes...you are holy..." I CRUSH THIS between my mortar and pestle.

[*the hero is trying to break free of her spell*]

What do you bring to me, anything of mettle, merit, or honor? I see through you like the glass that you are made of...grains of sand in the Wheel.

Do not worry, you will not be marred. You will be Destroyed! Unmade you will be, and born again you will! This is my half of the year, and I can see that the summer fires are spent. The hearth is cold, the sky grey and in this darkness I will peel the skin of your foolishness from your bones. Your skull I will weave into my necklace if it is worthy of a song, and from it I will drink my mead. What is left, I will compost, and see if I cannot draw forth something new that is worthy of the Maker.

This is my time…Time of the dead, of the ancestors, of the Fae, and of *your* ghosts. I hear them, *your* ghosts. They are all around us on this plain, swimming through thy blood and the song of your heart. They are calling you. What will you offer me? What will you offer to that which is beyond mortal conceptions? Listen, they call!

*[for a moment the hero is free and tries to follow the Fae]*

**The Fae:** [Fae speak, *sing-song as they weave through the audience*] Come! Come! The path is free and clear. Come! Come! The water is cold and pure! Come! Come! The door is open wide. Come! Come! The ancient ones inside! *[and back out of the audience]*

**Morrigu:** [*speaks*] I am eternal…is your soul strong enough to retain its flesh? *[the hero is battling with his shadow in the mirror]* Since the dawning of time, men have desired the pleasure and ecstasy that my womb can give, yet the fools refuse to see that I am both the womb and their tomb! Everything that is born will die and be renewed by my will.

Wars have been fought for eons for the rights to this sacred chamber of pleasure that is only mine. Wars fought, men fallen, and my laughter reigns on. *[laughter]* Heeheeheeehehehehehehehe hehee!!!!!! There is no king that may rule without my decree.

**Brigid:** [*emerging from the shadows with a light in hand, calmly speaks*] Hold, sister. *[the hero is frozen in place, trapped in time between the two goddesses]* It is true that this is your half of the year, but do remember that we share this power, this temple, this blood that courses through our veins. The Dream of Winter only makes the Oak

117

King stronger yet.   Do recall that my gift of fire to the hearth and poetry for the spirit is enough that any mortal may find peace in the darkest night of the year.

**Morrigu:** [*speaks begrudgingly*]  Aye, be that as it may be, but they will all come to me in the end. [*indicating the hero*]  He asked for truth.  I gave it to him.  Who does he think he was praying to and leaving offerings for?  It was I who created total obliteration.

One day, he will thank me for I gave him what he sought: destruction of lies woven within lies.  And now he grovels at my sacred cave seeking pleasures or boons!

**Brigid:** [*speaks*] Yes, but you have said it yourself: the end is just another beginning.  As summer heat calls the fruit to ripen, and winter coldness calls the seed to hardness, the return of the light of my fire calls the seed to life.  All may return to you, but they are born again through my breath in the Light of the Summerland.

**Morrigu:** [*speaks sarcastically*]  True indeed, Sister, but it is also true that these who robe themselves in the flesh, these mortals who carry only a drop of the essence of the gods, also bring with them all of their deceit, treachery, and fool-heartiness.   Watch them!   See how they make the same mistakes again and again!   And see how one lie spreads from one soul to the next like a plague, eating them from the inside out. There is nothing left for me but bones….

**Brigid:**  Your gift is in the giving and taking of life, and granting the power and aid of the Danu to those warriors on the battlefield who you see fit to rule the lands of Erin.

My gift is in the giving of Light and Inspiration.   In-spirit-elation, my torch burns bright in the eyes, hearts, and souls of humanity.   And it too spreads.   But not like fear or disease.   It spreads in love and jubilee.

So while your dark and cold lies like a mantle across the Earth, I will be the fire in the hearth keeping family and tribe warm.  I will be the inspiration, the ingenuity that flows in the blood of the bard, poet, storyteller, musician, mystic, priest, and priestess, that will lift the hearts of the weary, that they may sing at the Beltaine fires once more.

**Morrigu:** Sister, so true it is that you warm and brighten the hearts of many.   Yet I still hunger for a true warrior or a true lady who knows and will act from the truth of their core.   Look at him. He sees me through the mirror of his own projections.   His fear and rage twist the truth of who I am... Pure Surging LIFE FORCE  to be shaped by intent and will.  His warped vision twists me into something ugly and treacherous to be feared.  Look at him.  Warriors such as him find it easy to be angry....Yet, to muster the will to feel beyond the anger to what lies behind it... Aye, to deeply feel one's dark places...that takes true courage.   It is far easier to conquer thousands in battle than to conquer oneself.

Where are my spiritual warriors? Where are my activists willing to take a stand for life?

I grow impatient!    I look out into the sea of humanity... [*pointing and looking at the audience*]

[*THE CURSE OF THE MORRIGAN by Macha Nightmares - 2008*]

*"You who bring suffering to children:* May you look into the sweetest, most open eyes, and howl the loss of your innocence.

*You who ridicule the poor, the grieving, the lost, the fallen, the inarticulate, the wounded children in grown-up bodies:* May you look into each face, and see a mirror.   May all your cleverness fall into the abyss of your speechless grief, your secret hunger, may you look into that black hole with no name, and find....the most tender touch in the darkest night, the hand that reaches out.   May you take that hand. May you walk all your circles home at last, and coming home, know where you are.

*You tree-killers, you wasters:* May you breathe the bitter dust, may you thirst, may you walk hungry in the wastelands, the barren places you have made. And when you cannot walk one step further, may you see at your foot a single blade of grass, green, defiantly green. And may you be remade by its generosity.

*And those who are greedy in a time of famine*: May you be emptied out, may your hearts break not in half, but wide open in a thousand places, and may the waters of the world pour from each crevice, washing you clean.

*Those who mistake power for love*: May you know true loneliness. And when you think your loneliness will drive you mad, when you know you cannot bear it one more hour, may a line be cast to you, one shining, light woven strand of the Great Web glistening in the dark. And may you hold on for dear life.

*Those passive ones, those ones who force others to shape them, and then complain if it's not to your liking*: May you find yourself in the hard place with your back against the wall. And may you rage, rage until you find your will. And may you learn to shape yourself.

*And you who delight in exploiting others, imagining that you are better than they are:* May you wake up in a strange land as naked as the day you were born and thrice as raw. May you look into the eyes of any other soul, in your radiant need and terrible vulnerability. May you know your Self. And may you be blessed by that communion. And may you love well, thrice and thrice and thrice again and again and again.

May you find your face before you were born. And may you drink from deep, deep waters."

*FIND YOUR COURAGE, I BESEECH YOU!!! WHERE ARE MY WARRIORS???*

**The Fae:** [Fae-Speak, *while gesturing , seeking the "warriors", pointing, questioning, twittering, then weaving through the audience looking for the warriors and activists in Fae speak...thinking they found one then realizing they had not and moving on. They return to the hero and semi-circle around him, realizing he is a true warrior-*

*activist. Pointing at the hero, nodding, leaping in glee and jubilation and acknowledgement. Exiting gleefully, twittering].*

**Brigid:** [*speaks*] So I too speak, sister Morrigu, upon these sacred mountains of Katuah and Unaka, ancient current of the First Nations who once lived and prayed here.    Aye, yes, and the moon-faced people, the Yunweh T'sundi who dwell within the mountains, the Danu who arrived here on dragon ships from the lands of Erin. Come! Come! Listen to their song, as they rise from the deep.

[*The hero seems to be lifted by invisible strands by the Fae. They direct him with their "strings" and he becomes the medium to sing the ancient welcome song in honor of the Fae races dwelling here in Unaka.    After he sings, he collapses back into frozen time and the Fae disappear into the darkness again. Silence...then the Morrigu speaks.*]

**Morrigu:** [*speaks with power*] Then I shall speak first, since I sit at the beginning of the Wheel of the Year. I am life and death, beginning and end, the cup and the blade.   When your life looks ugly and shameful, and others fear you...heh!   Who is it who will be there for you?   It is I, the Morrigu.   It is I who will guide you through your transformations, even if I have to completely remake you. [*She kicks the hero over*]   Come ye forth then, riders of the eight winds and seasons.   Come ye forth and let us drink the nectar from my sacred cup!

[*lifts chalice*]   From the beginning of the dark of the year and the house of the ancestors, I ward the northwest, I grant life, I take life, and I renew life.

**Ward of the North (Nuada):** [*lifts sword*]   From the crowning of the Holly King, I ward the north, and I lay abundance upon thy hearth.

**Matron of the NE (Macha):** [*lights torch*]   From darkness and flame, I ward the northeast, and I rekindle the light that is forgotten beneath ice and snow.

**Ward of the East (Daghda):** [*stirs cauldron*]   Where sun and moon, day and night balance as one, I ward the east, and I strike true, that the way is clear of all obstructions.

**Matron of the SE (Brigid):** [*lifts multi-colored flame*]   From the altar of fertility, where the Lord & Lady couple as one, I ward the southeast, and I weave the tapestry of fate.

**Ward of the South (Manannán mac Lir):** [*brandishes stone of destiny*]   From the crowning of the Oak King, I ward the south. I strike away all illusions and ask, "what seeds have you sewn?"

**Matron of the SW (Áine):** [*displays basket contents*]   From heart to harvest, feast and becoming, I ward the southwest, and I offer you precisely what you have offered me.

**Ward of the West (Lugh):** [*holds spear aloft*]   Where moon and sun, night and day balance as one, I ward the west and wonder, when will you cross through the mists to the Summerlands?

**Morrigu:** [*speaks*] Yes, so we remember. We remember to cast the Circle whole, and open it that those benevolent beings whose time it is to speak may be heard.   I hear the Dragons above and below, they too have gathered here among us.   Welcome, ancient ones. Your guidance and wisdom are gratefully accepted.   Ahhhhhh, and the silence at the center of the storm. [*lights go out and silence for a 30 seconds*]

But I am the Queen of this night of All-Hallows-Eve. [*lights up*] I will clean your slate to write something new.   When your life looks ugly and shameful, and others fear you...heh!   When you even fear yourself...who is it who will be there for you? It is I, the Morrigu!   It is I who will guide you through your transformation, even if I have to completely remake you.

Who broke the trance of your life's contentment?   Who drove your passion like a spear through the boar of complacency?   Who calls you into the deep of the forests to pray and to sing, to drink deep from the sacred springs beneath beech, oak, and hazel?   Who wraps you in the sensual embrace and power of the moon on the banks of the ancient rivers?  It is I the Morrigu!  Who do you suppose was holding you when your world was crumbling around you?  Who laughed with you when your castle, built with shoddy stone, was left in nothing but ruins?

Yes, it was I, the Morrigu.

Could you not see again the stars, the sun, the moon, the forests, the mountains, the rivers, the vales, and those who loved you... waiting to help you smite that which no longer rang true on the anvil of the soul?

You called me! You! You poured ovations on my breasts and hearth.  You left your seeds on the landscape of my holy temple and now I DEMAND your true libations!

WAKE UP!!!!  [*Morrigu kicks through the back of the mirror*] See me, warrior!  See me for who I am and not what you want me to be.  I am the raven, death goes before me, and life springs up behind me.  I am the Queen of Samhain!  I am a battle goddess of the Danu, and I clear the field before me.  Do not invite me into your pleasures if you do not wish to see *all* of me.  I am the consort of kings, but crowns can be stripped away, for I am the temple within which they must pray.  I am the guardian of the gateway to the Summerland... [*the mirror via the two holders exit stage*],

Come find the mirror within.  Then, and only then, embrace me. Feel, f-e-e-l.  Yes, feel your anger and all your rage...[*Hero crying and feeling his pain*] and keep on feeling.  Surrender to that darkest place...go beyond your anger... Feel your sadness... your loneliness ....and the depths of your despair...Then, and ONLY then can your heart break open in LOVE.

Trust the arms of the Dark Goddess to catch you.  My dear, in the fear to surrender to your feelings the pain is only prolonged. [*Hero falls to floor and the Morrigu catches him he looks up into Her eyes and finally sees Her and himself*]  Surrender to the Void,

123

surrender to my Love.   It is only then that you will truly see me…and truly see yourself.

[*whispered*]  Surrender to me and be reborn. [**Lights Out** for *30 seconds.*]

Stand Warrior! [*Morrigu lifts him to his feet*]    Stand in the strength and honor of your heritage, and I will guide you on the spiral path through the labyrinth of your internal landscape.   Stand, like the oak and go deep into the dark of the year…keep your fires warm, and rise, newly forged with the dawning of spring. My sister, Brigid, will be there to send you onward…ever onward through the pathways of the soul.

This is the beginning of the Dark of the Year, a time to journey within and reflect on the internal garden…what seeds have you harvested from this year in passing? What will you plan for the garden of your soul for years to come? Will you continue to sew only annual crops, or gathering the leavings and weeds of others' gardens? Or will you plant a garden that will last for all of eternity upon the landscape of your soul?

**Brigid:** [*speaks*] My light is bright and my river is swift and clear, but methinks it will not come so easily to those who navigate the rivers of the gods. What is in the hearts of humanity, what seeds they choose to sew is entirely of their own volition…I can only inspire, and intend that the flame that I hold high in the flower of winter darkness will guide them into safe harbor and lead to deep penetration of their roots into fertile soil.

**The Fae:** [*sing Fae-song as they weave through the audience and back out of the audience, bringing the hero with them*]

**Brigid:** [*speaks*] Perhaps the Lords and Ladies of the ancient halls of the gods can help me call these mortals into awakening?

**Nuada:** [*speaks*] Ho! Ho! What happens here, under my reign? For am I not still king here? I will not have blood and carnage upon thy hearth!

**Morrigu:** [*speaks*] Worry not, my lover, Grey King of the North, for it is not flesh I seek to devour, but it is the death of stagnant spirit.

**Nuada:** [*speaks*] So what goes? Come, the veil is parting on this night of the Morrigu's keeping. Samhain...the doorways to the Summerlands are open. I will ward these lands and protect them from all that is malevolent and malicious. Let us raise together a cone of power, to protect and yet invite in those beings that would come to the aid of those who have gathered here in this forest temple. [*weaves a web of energy into a cone of power, drawing from all the elements which have been gathered; the Fae reenter with the hero now transformed*]

Where do I dance and whose mountains will tremble? WHOSE MOUNTAINS WILL TREMBLE? Where is the Wildman? Where is Ing? Come forth! Ride the north winds!!!

**The Fae:** [*chant with musicians*] Ing! Ing! Ing! [*enter Wildman in wild dancing fervor*]

**Morrigu:** [*speaks*] Ahhhhh, and where is my Innah? Who will dance thru time with me? Wildwoman of the forest, come, unleash your voice! Sing your ancient song!

**The Fae:** [*chant with musicians*] Innah! Innah! Innah! [*enter Wildwoman in wild dance*]

**Brigid:** [*speaks*] The Lord and Lady are among us. We will invite all to dance and move freely...to shake off the shackles of the soul, find the source within of eternal light and one's true nature. You have made your offering within the veil of the goddess. Listen to the voices of the Triple Goddess...the light is born in the darkness; the darkness is born in the light!

**The Fae:** [*sing-song as they weave through the audience*] Beware! Take heed! The night of the Fae is swelling. Turn on! Go deep! The house of the goddess is calling!

The ghosts and ancestors are here among us! The elementals and ascended ones are here among us. Saints and sages are here among us. Take heed!

**Morrigu:** [*speaks*] To the Sword and Raven!

**Brigid:** [*speaks*] To the Fire and Hammer!

**The Fae:** [*sing-song as they weave through the audience lifting people to dance*] Rise! Rise! Trom-bon the witching drums of transformation. Sound the horns in the granite and watch the mountains rise and fall like the waves on the ocean. Drink the reins of destiny. Swell and rise. The tide is pulling on the shore of our hearts. Destroy us! Erode away that which no longer serves. Make us anew! Shore up that which is worth keeping, that the rest can be cast away.

Let us sit at the table of the gods on this one night! Weave us into your tapestry, sweet, sweet Lady, that our story can be seen and heard in the halls of the gods in all time. Let us remember what we came here for and throw the rest away.

**Nuada:** [*speaks*] Rise! Rise! [*Wildman and Wildwoman are drawing people into the dance with much fervor and animation*] Rise and dance like you have never danced before. Let your sweat run like a river. Let your masks and costumes slip away into the nothingness that they are, that we can stand naked before the piercing eyes of the goddess. She sees through you! Dance it off! Dance off all the shame, the hurt, the game, the nothingness. Rise! Rise and Dance!

**The Fae:** [Fae speak, *sing-song as they weave through the audience driving people to dance harder*] Cast the rest away! There is nothing here but your heart beat. External. Internal. BOOM! Rise up! No one is going to do it for you! This is your life! Your life! A wink in the eyes of the gods…BOOM! Rise up! Dance! Let the fervor of ecstasy and wildness wash over you like a hot desert wind. Dance. Dance and be free like you will live for this moment alone and then pass on into the Summerlands.

**Morrigu & Brigid:** [*speak*] The Circle is cast; this space is sacred and burning for you to sweat your tears into the earth. Return! Return! Return! [*"Return" becomes as chant, slowly quieting as the music builds into oscillating peaks for the rest of the ritual*]

[*The Fae are stirring up the audience with the Wildman and Wildwoman, driving them all to dance...finding the outsiders and drawing them within to the hottest part of the dance. No one is left to rot in complacency. Music continues to ebb and flow until all merry makers are satiated. At the end of the evening celebrations, the hero will once again become animated by the Fae as he sings the leaving song....*]

**The Hero:** [*singing* Hush o' Babe (tradition Irish folk), *followed by*] We bring this circle to a close...to all the spirits and beings who have gathered here to our aid, go if you must...stay if you will... and come again when we call...know that you always have a home here in our circle. Blessed be...

# The Last Song of the Hemlocks

Winter. She tears at the ego like a rabid wildcat slashing her way through a flock of placid sheep. She has pulled all of the leaves from the branches and left all naked in the cold, reaching to the belt of Orion for illumination and promise. This is the time of sculpting. Her claws and teeth rake the mountains, rearranging the landscape both within and around, and new ghosts arise from her carnage, toying with all who think they are secure in their holdings. Dragon winds whip the mountains into shape; their icy breath sheathes all creatures with a beating heart in a blanket of white.

"Go inside," they whisper through the high branches of beech and oak, "go inside to your roots, whilst we throw ice, trees, and branches. This is our time. Go inside."

The Fae huddle under the roots of ancient trees, in dry caves, or within great halls of timber and stone, where the roaring fires in the hearths hark back to Summer's cheer, liberating the ice dragons and Lady Winter to attend to their own outdoor festivities. Over the hearth fires, kettles and cauldrons boil with life. The smells of the long-past harvest and the recent hunt dance in lazy, wafting circles around the heads of those who have gathered. Outside, the booming music of the ice dragons at play with the roof and neighboring pines are only another extension of the inner orchestra.

Laughter is thick and rich like the blood-pudding in the oven. Tongues are loosened with honey wine, unfurling stories and merry songs. The voices that dance upon the tongues vie for position in the room, bumping into one another, wrestling, clambering over one another, and twisting into a raucous fervor that would make any Celt smile. The tongues, which are most often connected to a head found resting securely upon a body, wander over near the hearth for warmth and to roll out the stories of summer, forgotten ages, heroes, and heroines.

"Come, sister! Let us invite the milk out of the hazelnuts with the mortar and pestle. The kettle is hot and the water within would draw the stories out of the sacred nuts, and wake the bard from his sleep."

An incessant chuckle of laughter erupts from near the fire, not unlike the boiling of the bear stew in the cauldron. It ripples across the hall, eddying around the towering timbers holding the roof and snow in check, and sloshing the wagging tongues back into the heads within which they belonged. With the tongues at bay, smiles begin to light up the room from behind thick beards, long braids, and feathers. The hall is then quiet, other than the sounds of Lady Winter and her marauding hordes outside. Steaming cups of hazelnut tea are passed around. Silently, all hold their cups, warming their hands and reflecting on the sweet earthy aroma. Even the children hold their tongues and sit in stillness.

One of the Grandfather's begins to speak, "We have gathered here since the Dawn of the Danu upon these shores, and so we shall until her dusk. Even then I imagine we will still gather here, if the Old Ones and the Unseen allow it."

He turns to a human skull on the mantle above the fire, "Many have walked in and out of different houses. We come, we go. We come again. It is the way it has always been. Just as the bear is returned again to the Mother in the cauldron's stew, he is born again within us, helping our kin grow stronger. He will tell us his stories in our bodies, and yet laze about in the Summer Country before coming again to walk amongst us and the forested hills."

Heads were nodding in agreement. The delicious scent of the stew, the pudding, and cooling loaves of homemade bread lay like a warm blanket across everyone's hearts. The yet untouched hazelnut tea is towing at everyone's discipline, saying, "Drink me!"

All knew that is was not yet time, so they hold their temptation at bay.

The Grandfather sits down.    In his place stands one of the Grandmothers, and she speaks, "And since the beginning, it has been so, the coming and going of the soul.    Each body is shed like a skin of a snake.    Sometimes we remember, sometimes we do not, depending on one's accomplishments in the life before.

"Listen to Lady Winter outside this hall.  Her minions are carving out new stories that many of us will not see until the first flower. And so too she carves us within each lifetime and the turning of the Great Wheel."

She sits down with some of her granddaughters near the fire. They cuddle against her, each sending silent prayers to Danu, mother of the Golden Ones, that when they became young mothers, their Grandmother's soul may be reborn into the world through their womb.    That is of course, once she passes over into the Summer Country and stirred into the Dagda's cauldron.

The youngest of the children looks to her mother as if to ask, "May I drink the hazelnut tea now?"

The mother shakes her head, saying silently, "No, it is not yet time."

A young couple then stands, with the hero's light glowing on each of their brows, and walk quietly and nobly to the hearth.   From the mantle, they respectfully lift the human skull together, she with her left hand and he with his right, and turn together to face their kin.

First speaks the young lady, "Since the beginning, the Lord and Lady have walked as One.   At times seeming to be only one God or Goddess, at other times as many Gods who are often at odds with one another through their human children.   Tonight, the Lord and Lady stand as one."

Then speaks the young lord, "And so we pour the river of our combined knowledge and strength into the house of our ancestor."

They raise the skull to the timbered roof and pour their own cups of hazelnut tea into the skull.   Outside, the wind plays wildly with chimes hanging from timbers and Hawthorne branches.   The ice dragons cast their breath across the solid oak doors to the hall - though otherwise sealed against the forays of Winter's hordes. For a moment, a noticeable chill spirals down the timbers in the hall, races across the floor, snakes up the limbs of the couple, and settles within the skull.   The children burrow closer into the laps of their parents and grandparents, peering out with wide eyes from under blankets and cloaks.

The couple turns to the fire, pouring a portion of the hazelnut tea into the flames and a portion into the stew. With their backs turned to their kin, no one can see what is revealed to them in the flames. A silence deeper than any snow holds the room in a tense web. No one moves. No one makes a sound. Even the breath seems to step outside of time. If an unknowing visitor would open the doors to the hall in this moment, it is likely all would shatter like a sculpture of ice and dust, blown away into nothingness.

After the frozen silence, the couple turn *deiseil* back to their kin with glowing eyes, and speak together, "May our ancestors come again amongst us.  May our forefather, Oisín, the river of our lore in this tea of hazel, come amongst us now as we drink. Welcome Oisín, weaver and word-smith. You and your craft are welcome here among us. Come sit by our hearth fire."

Radiating a golden warmth and beauty, summer rushes back into the hall via the hearth and banishes winter to the outdoors.  As the couple drinks the hazel nut tea from Oisín's skull, the warmth washes through them like birdsong, filling the air with spiraling rainbow Celtic knots weaving ghosts of constellations that will not be seen in a clear night sky for many months yet to come. The children clap and wiggle, while mothers nod ascent, "Yes, it is time to drink the tea."

The warm tea washes the last remnants of winter back from the mountains of their minds, opening the door to revelry, merry making, wrestling, and feasting. Grandmothers and older children begin to set the great table of oak with tray after tray of steaming boar and goose, simmering bear stew, mountains of roasted roots and winter greens, plates of hot breads, and freshly churned butter. Elders look to the windows at the scourging white winds, sharing memories of the ancient oak tree that had become the great table several generations before. It is known amongst them that the oak had been planted by Oisín before his fairy lover had carted him off to Tír na nÓg. He had tended the grove with verse, song, craft, steel, and the lore of the Fianna. The grove still sings through the generations and the seasons, calling to those who can still listen to the ancient tongue of the unseen.

Children and fathers tumble on the floor with one another in a bray of chaos, giggling, laughter, and tears. Arms and legs knot into various contortions that leaves one to wonder if the clans' war-craft and play were the vary models for the Celtic knots adorning the hall timbers. A visible end in the continuous stream of bodies tumbling cannot be found until one of the grandmothers begins banging on a pot to announce that the meal was ready. Everyone scrambles to their seats as another silence settles across the hall. The bounty set before them dampens the flapping of tongues and the jostling of elbows amongst the children.

With the silence, returns the reverence for winter and the temporary summer housed in the great hall. Eyes meet across the table. All feasters hope on this eve - just as lightning and winter storms had begun the ancient oak's journey to become the clan's table - that the genius of their ancestors and Oisín will infuse them with otherworldly wisdom, to light their way through the dark of the year. Most years, Oisín would embody as bard and storyteller through one of the family members, drawing everyone together for lore and word-craft until the sun came again in the morning.

Yet on this Midwinter's eve, the feast is only just beginning, when a girl-child screams like a wildcat and jumps onto the table, spilling bowls and platters of food everywhere. Her father tries to grab for her, but one of the grandmother's cries over the din of shouting, "Stop! It is Oisín. I see his light upon her brow."

Everyone quiets down and settles uneasily back into their seats. Usually, Oisín waits until well after the feast to arrive, when folk had gathered by the hearth to tell stories, share memories, and plan for the coming warm season.

We are listening, ancestor," speaks the Grandmother, "you are welcome here amongst us. Merry meet!"

Oisín smiles through the eyes of the girl-child. When he speaks, it is as if in song. Faint bells and chimes chatter around his words in the rafters above, and unseen harp music begins to vibrate from the wood grain in the oak and beech timbers of the hall. Together, with the words of the ancient one speaking, this rich tapestry of sound holds everyone spellbound. Never a pause in the weaving of the current, and soon all are drifting on the tide of Oisín's craft.

And his words wove through the tongue of the young maiden, "Come again we are to the end of an age. Great ones tower and fall, feeding the lesser. The lesser, unknowing that their feast is short sighted and borrowed from the future, scramble for the leavings of a dying beast and giants who have long slumbered. Yet the feast will soon end. Coyotes will walk amongst the landscape, cleaning the world of debris and refuse. Wolves will chase down the weak, whilst hosts of the Otherworld will strive to keep dark things at bay."

Everyone ceases eating and is bound to the streams of music twined into the tongue of their young kin.

"It is time to awaken the trees who slumber. The Age of the Hemlock has come to an end. Many will move on to the Summer Country and few will remain among us. The ward of the Hemlock has shared with me a riddle, which is a song, which is a key and a door. And so it should be remembered as the *Last Song of the Hemlock*."

He is silent for a moment; it seems as if the girl-child is standing frozen on the table. A soft silence settles on the hall, like the warm, thick silence before a summer storm crashes into the mountains with unruliness and fervor. Somewhere in the winter forest, deep in the mountain, a single drum begins to call, as if a softened wing percussing upon a hollow log.

"Thump, thump, thump, thump, thump," says the drum, and repeating, like a gentle thunder in the distance. The spiraling song of a flute begins to work its way through the cracks around the doors of the hall, and snake its way inside and across the floor. Then like rain, the flute washes over the hall in mournful wailing, like a ghost who lost her lover centuries before.

The marrow of everyone's bones shimmers in longing for places unseen, dreams overlooked, for a few drops of the Light of Erin, and the rejuvenation that comes between lives in the Summer Country. Oisín's voice emerges like a screech owl's call from across a deep cove through the mist of the flute and gentle thunder of the drum... eerily and from another world that is brighter and darker than this one.

*A flute calls deep from the Forest,*
*Followed by echoing drum.*
*Hark to the sound of the Piper,*
*For Fae-blood runs deep in your bones.*

*Follow the winding mushroom trail*
*To the door of the Beech'n Queen.*
*Knock quietly upon her barren feet,*
*For surely she will let you in.*

*Tip-toe across the flowers,*
*Laugh yourself across the glen,*
*For hear the Stone People speak at last*
*In the same language as men.*

*Jeremy Schewe*

*A white horse a'waits at the Mountain,*
*A Grey King rests upon his steed.*
*Fiobahr is stirring his Cauldron.*
*Nuada is spreading his seed*

*So tie your hair me darlin'*
*In a long-spun golden braid.*
*Close your eyes me darlin'*
*We're off to the sweet Summerland.*

*Music calls from the Forest –*
    *Hurry on bare feet and see.*
*Away up high on the Mountain,*
*Come a dancing with the Fairy.*

*The veil is thin as an oak tree,*
*And a rainbow will bring you inside*
*Laugh your way up the Mountain,*
*Leaving behind your pride.*

*Circle around the Lake shore,*
*Three times maybe five,*
    *And dance within the center*
*For maybe then you'll find*

*That a white horse a'waits at the Mountain,*
*A Grey King rests upon his steed.*
*Fiobahr is stirring his Cauldron.*
*Nuada is spreading his seed*

*So tie your hair me darlin'*
*In a long-spun golden braid.*
*Close your eyes me darlin'*
*We're off to the sweet Summerland.*

*Music calls from the Forest –*
*Hurry on bare feet and see.*
*Away up high on the Mountain,*
*Come a dancing with the Fairy.*

When the song closes, everyone sits silently. Oisín is gone and the Otherworldly music with him. The fire needs to be fed, cooling food eaten, dishes washed, and the children put to bed. The little girl-child, whom Oisín's river swept through so suddenly, lies sleeping on the table. The gentle rumbling of her snoring, like distant thunder, is the only sound in the hall.

# Middle Eastern

# Euphrosyne of Trebizond

Her tongue ran gently along the inside of her lips, pushing back the dry night air. The sand beneath her still radiated the sun's warmth from the day through the carpet beneath her thighs and buttocks. All of the servants were asleep in other tents with the exception of Marcus, who stood guard outside of her tent.  An evening breeze lifted the burgundy silk door coverings in teasing play. Euphrosyne slowly opened her eyes partially into crescent slivers.

əΨc

Outside, the full moon was setting.  Its reflection danced on the face of the Tigris. The Wind blowing across the desert was silent, for there were few obstacles to impede its movement.  Yet, the Wind could reach its invisible fingers, long and probing across the ancient river bed and find the ruins of the ancient walls of Nineveh. And if he was willing to stretch his advantage, the Wind could reach across the low hillock to the remains of the ancient city's Mashki Gate.  There he could play with the silk walls and door of the visitors in a way he had not had the opportunity to in almost a thousand years.

Lighting his fingers on the fringes of the richly embroidered silks, the Wind sighed in anticipation; seeing all and seeing nothing. With patience, he could slide along the rolled out Persian carpet within, or across the ripples in the roof, and wrap his arms gently around first the ankles and thighs, then around the abdomen and breasts.  If the Wind was patient enough, he could slide along the shoulders, neck, ears, and lips of the most perfect reflection of the goddess.

əΨc

Euphrosyne opened her eyes completely.  She was no longer alone.  She could feel his presence nearing as she could when she was a little girl.  The wind had broken her reverie, sliding beneath her

141

night dress and lifting her long brown hair like seaweed over her high cheek bones and full lips.  It had been over three years since she had seen her friend and childhood love, Cadwalch of Angora.  And just as when she was a child and adolescent, she knew he was close even now.  Her spine was tingling and she sat up erect.  A fire ran through her feet and hands, almost as if they had fallen asleep, but more so as if they had been asleep for eons and were just now being filled with life.

"Rise up, come to me," the Wind seemed to beckon.

The silk door panels were lifted once again by the breeze, almost to the point where they hovered parallel to the plain of the river.  The moon danced on the water in expectation.

Euphrosyne could hardly remember her father's face, much less that of Cadwalch, but she remembered his presence.  She remembered the day, over three years ago, when the Qara Koyunlu rode over the mountains and down toward her father's city in Anatolia on the Black Sea.  Trebizond was a proud and rich city, but it was completely at the mercy of either the Byzantine knights or the Turkish Shi'ites, depending on who had the current upper hand on the control of the trade routes in the region.  And when the son of the Qara Koyunlu, rode into the city's main gates with thousands of horseman behind him, the young Euphrosyne thought nothing of it.  At least once a year the Qara came riding to collect the agreed tribute from her father Alexios IV before riding west to Angora, and then in their circuitous route through tribute paying kingdoms before turning south to their capital Tabriz, in Assyria.

She knew that her father had been strengthening political ties with other regional powers.  Most of her sisters were engaged or married to Italian and Greek princes throughout the Aegean, Anatolia, and Venice.  The Orthodox family had survived on maintaining good political ties, yet she could hardly stomach the news when her mother told her she was to marry, Muzaffer al-Dinn Jahan Shah, son of Qara Yusuf, the tribal leader of the Koyunlu.

She remembered feeling as if her guts had been torn out and her heart locked into a casket of ice. She could not cry, for a princess of the Trebizond line would not cry. But inside she wept oceans of tears for her misfortune. Not only would this marriage mean that she would be married to a radical Shi'ite who lived hundreds and hundreds of miles away from her family via unsafe land routes, but that she also could never see her dear Cadwalch again. She had truly hoped that her father would agree to the request of the Lords of Angora to marry her and Cadwalch in the effort to further bolster the political ties between the two great cities.

A smile cracked her dry lips. Here she was now, traveling by land, secretly, with her small entourage back to Anatolia, waiting at the ancient city ruins of Nineveh. This rendezvous was at the request of Cadwalch as he had instructed in the last of their secret letters.

The wind slid once again through her silk night dress sending shivers up her spine. The wedding to Jahan Shah had been a blur, but the night after the wedding, when he had come to her chambers to claim her as his bride, her life changed forever.

Later that year, Qara Yusuf died and Jahan Shah's brother, Iskander became the new tribal leader. Jahan Shah, as a potential rival to the throne, was not safe in Tabriz any longer, so he and his entourage, including Euphrosyne and her servants, fled to Baghdad where another brother reigned over the city, independent from the rest of Qara Iskander's domain. Though further inland than Tabriz, Baghdad was an exciting change for Euphrosyne for many reasons. As a city, it was much larger than Tabriz, and because of the Tigris River trade routes down to the Red Sea, she could once again visit the ocean, albeit not the Mediterranean or the Black, but she felt closer to home then she had in almost a year.

Things changed for her again that year. First, Niccolò de Conti-Crispo, the Venetian husband of one of her sisters, came to visit Euphrosyne on a trading expedition. Second, he planned to embark on one of the ships in a massive fleet of Chinese treasure ships commanded by a Muslim eunuch, Admiral Zheng He. De Conti-

Crispo saw this as an excellent opportunity to find a more efficient trade route to China other than the Silk Road. While he was staying in Baghdad, de Conti-Crispo and Zheng He persuaded Jahan Shah to embark as well. Stories of the wealth and power of the new emperor of China had long since reached the ears of traders and those of power, or of those who sought power. Emperor Zhu Di of the newly established Ming Dynasty was planning the coronation of the millennia and was entertaining royal guests and showering them with wealth, feasts, and pleasures beyond their wildest dreams.

For two years, Jahan Shah was overseas in China. During that time, Euphrosyne began having secret correspondence via letters with Cadwalch in Angora. It was not, however, until Jahan Shah returned from Beijing in 1422 with his pregnant Cantonese concubine, that Euphrosyne's and Cadwalch's letters became conspiratory. It was not that Jahan was any less disrespectful than before he traveled to China, or that he was necessarily abusive that spawned the formulation of her plans to escape, but it was that he ignored her altogether and doted on his Cantonese woman.

As planned, she had slipped out at the new moon in the month of Safar, with only her most trusted servants and guards who had come with her from Trebizond. Markus, the captain of her guard, had long been her father's friend, and had communicated via secret dispatch with Alexios as to the planned escape. Nothing was ever heard back from her father, but Cadwalch was willing to hide them in Angora and had made all of the necessary plans for them.

The ride north had been thrilling to Euphrosyne. To feel the strength of a stallion between her legs again, sweating as it trotted and ran across the desert under the dark of the moon. It was exhilarating to feel the power of her people surging through her limbs each night as they rode north from Baghdad along the east bank of the Tigris. As they rode, the layers of the Shi'ite fundamental beliefs of women, and the discredit that Jahan Shah had paid her, peeled off of her like layer upon layer of sea salt-crusted silks.

"I pray for that poor Cantonese woman," she remembered thinking, as she had ridden hard for two weeks, "may Grace guide her home."

She stood up in the tent and walked to the door to look outside. The wind lifted the burgundy silk door caressingly to her right cheek and wrapping around her breast, momentarily stirring a desire in her that she had only allowed herself to feel in dreams.

"Markus, I believe that he is here," she said.

"Yes, my lady. His horses and knights crossed the Tigris a few moments ago," the guard replied.

She turned back to the center of her tent. Setting each foot in front of the other very slowly, wondering how she would embrace this friend that she had not seen in over three years. She found again her warm seat on the carpet, turning once again to face the door and close her eyes.

The warmth of the sand brought her body awareness to the backs of her thighs, buttocks, and yoni pressed against the earth. The sand and earth answered her presence and pressed back against her. A gentle rhythm of undulating pressure between her body and the earth pulsed between her breathing. Like a bond or seal of antiquity pressed into warm wax, her consciousness slid into the earth.

Outside, two lions roared to one another in the distance. The echo of the lions on the Tigris caught the reflection of the moonlight and crept through the tent flaps on the back of the Wind. Like a hawk who knows its prey, the echo of the lions' roar pierced into her inner ears, and scrambled the lines of time in its grip.

As she came to, she found herself, or a reflection of herself, in a wide temple filled with her priestesses, serving the partialities of the goddess so revered in Nineveh. The Tigris, whose very limbs could drive a man to madness and desire, was pulsing with the spring floods from the snowmelt in the mountains to the north. She stepped down from her dais, her gold-dusted, nude flesh shimmering in the midday sun. He had come to her with his answer. She could see him making his way through the writhing bodies and limbs in a hundred forms of pleasure.

His face was stoic and stern. He nodded to the elegant blonde priestess from Thule who greeted him at the foot of her dais. Then he stepped past her, for now his eyes saw nothing but she who descended towards him in all of her golden glory: she, whom all men and gods desire; she, whose perfection in flesh and the arts of pleasure haunted dreams, both sleeping and waking; she, who is the goddess of fertility, war, and love; she who is the Morning and Evening Star. He came to the foot of her dais and stood several paces from her.

"My lady," he said, without the usual obeisance that men and women gave her.

She looked him up and down, burrowing into the depths of his eyes with her gaze. "What is your answer then, Gilgamesh?"

And he answered thus, "Woe to him whom Ishtar has honored. The fickle goddess treats her passing lovers cruelly, and the unhappy wretches usually pay dearly for the favors heaped upon them. Animals, enslaved by love, lose their native vigor: they fall into traps laid by men or are domesticated by them. She has loved the Lion, mighty in strength, and dug for him seven within seven pits. She has loved the steed, proud in battle, and destined him for the halter, goad, and whip. For her love is fatal. I know of your desire for Tammuz, Lord of the harvest, and how this love caused his untimely death. My life is but my own, and mine own answer to you is that I will not be your lover."

With that, he turned his back to her and began to walk away.

"No one turns their back on me or says no to my pleasures," She cried.

The echo of her voice crashed through the lovers throughout the temple, freezing them, cutting through all pleasures, and squeezing time to a standstill within the vice of her voice, with the exception of Gilgamesh, who continued to walk determinedly away.

"Come back here!"

He continued out the temple gate towards the Tigris.

Turning to the heavens in her rage, she cried out, "Father! Give me the Bull of Heaven so that I may destroy this man who has refused me!"

It is with great sadness that Anu instilled this boon upon his daughter, knowing that the Bull cannot be controlled. Gilgamesh escaped the wrath of the Bull in the scuffle that ensued, but his friend and compatriot, Enkidu was slain. In response, Gilgamesh captured the Bull and took it with him to Byzantium. In the market of this great city, he traded the Bull for Helvetii iron to a Volcae tribal leader, who hailed from the headwaters of the Danube in the ancient Hercynian Forest.

Over the years, the Bull became the icon of the Volcae Celts, and desiring more than anything to return to Assyria and the pastures of Anu, the Bull instilled restlessness in the Volcae. They became known as the Tectosagii, or the "land grabbers" to the rest of the civilized world, for the Bull led some of them on a wild territory conquest across southern Gallia and Cisalpina to the west and south. And further, the Bull led the majority of the Tectosagii across Macedonia and Arcadia to destroy Delphi. They crushed the ancient people of Byzantium. And they eventually settled into the highlands of Anatolia before they finally grew wise enough to trade the Bull with the Scythians. The Bull completed his revenge on Ishtar, by driving the same wildness into the Scythians as he did the Tectosagii Celts. The Scythians fire could not be tempered until the destruction of Nineveh was complete.

Outside, another roar from one of the lions shattered Euphrosyne from the boundaries of her vision. She could hear the heated breath of a bull outside of her tent. As her head cleared and she could listen more closely, she recognized that it was not a bull at all, but it was the panting of an exhausted stallion.

Fragments of the vision still lingered in the periphery of her mind as she struggled to find the life current that she presently inhabited. She felt almost as if she was suspended in a vast spider's web. Each of the strands trailed off to some distant land that her ancestors came from, or perhaps Jahan's, Markus's, Cadwalch's, or many other unseen faces or hands connected to her present state. Here she sat in the middle. The web of fate was stretched across her and she had placed herself willingly within its grasp. Perhaps fate had seen it otherwise, and had dragged her here knowingly. She could not know whether it was the crafting of the Sun, the Moon, the Lion, the Bull, the Lamb, or the Morning Star. She could not obtain this knowledge and never would. Yet, only she could make the choice of whether she was going to be trapped in the web, or if she could release herself from invisible bondage.

"No!" she cried, opening her eyes just as the moon set over the horizon.

She jumped quickly to her feet in the new darkness and crashed headlong into the sweating chest of a man entering her tent. Her scream was stifled by his warm hand across her mouth. His other arm snaked around the small of her back and pulled her closer to his chest.

"Euphrosyne, it is me, Cadwalch. I am here."

Looking up in the darkness, trying to make out his features, she surrendered her body's tension. He let his right hand down from her mouth and traced his fingers gently along her chin to her left ear. In the darkness, their eyes found one another. The whites of their eyes were remnants of the moon reflecting on the Tigris. Deeply they looked into the oasis of the souls that lie within and behind the other, finding the sanctuary of ancient friendship and stories left untold. Like the windows of a great cathedral, they let the light of their souls shine through the windows to illuminate the sanctuary within.

His hands traced the line from the top of her right ear, across her eyebrow and pressed gently into the center of her brow.

"I see you," he said.

"And I see you," she replied.

Their lips opened to one another in a kiss that they had hungered for what seemed like eternity and yet never known. Her dried lips parted to his and soon their lips were dry no more, for their wandering hands were enough to draw water from the driest of Nineveh's abandoned wells and to bring rain to the driest of deserts.

ꙋΨꙅ

Outside, the lion and the lioness lay curled around one another. In the distance, another lion called to his mate. The Wind cut through the ruins of Nineveh with the ecstatic howling of brazen lovers healing the gulf of a thousand years, braided with the soft hissing of tussled silks, and mixed with the Wind's silent and eternal voice.

# Hathor's Dreamscape

In his dream, he woke shaking in the sarcophagus. He shared the king's chamber with his father in the Great Pyramid of Giza. Through heavy stone and looming darkness, he watched the full moon rise over the silhouettes of palms, the Sphinx, and the Nile. Very few clouds were present. The horned goddess, Hathor, called to him within the silver light of the rising moon.

He found his feet carrying him in a passage absent of light to the surface, where night lay freshly across the desert and warm sands from the day's heat welcomed his bare feet. Hathor's beckoning was easy to follow across the sands, for a perfume hung in the air along her lavender trail. The trail became a railroad track, along which his feet seemed to be carrying him towards a town. In the back of his mind, he knew he was going to this town to buy a Playboy magazine.

"Hathor, where are you taking me," he thought.

No answer, only allusive moonlight illuminating the railroad tracks.

As his feet brought him closer to town, he felt like a jellyfish being carried along by a current that he had little control over. His feet were being directed by another as if he was remote controlled, and with inner vision he could see the Nile, like a river of fertility carrying him in its course through the eye of an ankh. The current drew him on. Invisible tendrils reached for him, curling around his loins and thighs, probing little rootlets into surface of his mind, and refusing to let go.

"What am I doing," he thought. "I am wasting my time, energy, and money in this trivial pursuit."

In observation of his surroundings as he entered the town, box stores and multi-national corporations were sucking people's energy away as fast as they could regenerate the essence to replace it.

"No more," he cried, breaking the grasping vines from his limbs.

Tearing the rootlets from his mind was no easy task. They had taken hold and were digging into his cortex. He pulled and it felt like fire ripping through his mind, burning and stabbing, for the roots did not want to let go. He pulled until he felt like he was dragging his head through barbed wire, and pouring boiling water into the open wounds. He pulled until every last rootlet came ripping out with a bone-shivering scream of agony. Turning from the railroad, he stumbled across the sands blindly, humming madly to himself to cool his burning crown. Everything went black.

As the sun rose through the darkness of the Hercynian Forest, he found that his feet were drawing him through the ancient wood towards his home. As his feet pressed into wet autumn leaves, he could see the Morning Star on the horizon in front of him. The canopy of the forest loomed over the path, like a gothic cathedral, each trunk a pillar holding up the vastness of the heavens. The emerging stars were the only fresco to gaze upon. The complexity of the masterpiece swam through his vision as the individual stars were winking at him through the spreading capillary branches.

A chill ran down his spine. He looked around and could see nothing that would conjure this disturbing premonition, but he could feel eyes watching him. The hairs on his arms and neck never lied. Stopping in place, he looked around for something to use as a weapon. Anything would do; a rock, a stick, an old log. Anything would do. But as he looked for something to grab, he noticed a cerulean glow on the forest floor around his feet. He turned to the east, and saw the moon winking at him through the trees. His breath caught for a moment. Hathor streaked by him again with swollen breasts dripping with milk. The milk clouded his eyes and he felt himself falling.

He was trying to unstrap a crate from the inside of a moving airplane. The deafening sounds of explosions all around the Boeing B-17 Flying Fortress reminded him that he was in grave danger. The

World War II bomber was on a run dropping bombs over a darkened city. Yet, the plane was hardly in one piece, as surface to air guns ripped holes in the floor and walls. The pilot was hit and the plane folded in upon itself and broke apart. The steel floor folded towards the earth before him when he was struck in the back of the head by a bomb rack falling into the abyss. The air pressure crushed him as he fell, only half conscious of childhood memories in Cornwall flashing through him until stillness.

Opening his eyes, the plane was quite calm, as it was the private jet of a pleasant, middle-aged blond woman with her family. She smiled at him. Her eyes were bright, and with his second sight knew that she was pregnant.

He stood to walk toward her and found himself inside a genetic laboratory. The first tank he came to contained some malformed babies. There were two of them together. One was shaped like an eggplant; the other was mentally a vegetable and red like a tomato. He picked up the eggplant child, partly in horror and partly in compassion, when the obviously disturbed parent-scientist-DNA donors ran quickly into the lab and tore the child from his arms. He was reprimanded heavily, but before he could apologize, the plane was hit by rapid fire from an enemy fighter plane. He was jerked back to his knees and the middle-aged blond woman smiled at him knowingly. As the plane caught fire, the sun radiated in her eyes.

The plane wavered as it descended quickly. The pilot was fighting to keep control of the failing steering, while fire and smoke trailed behind. The plane leveled enough to thread between two western cedars in a grove of ancient trees that were several thousand feet tall. The softened crash brought them to the forest floor among ferns and salmon berries.

He popped the round emergency hatch to crawl out onto the wing of the plane. When he stood up, he was inside the kitchen of a forest gnome. Shelves were covered with little clay plates, cups, and utensils of wood. A kettle was boiling over the fire. The gnome whistled to himself as he set the table, occasionally wiping his hands off on his dirty white apron. There was tea, bread, cheese, and some cold slices of salt-dried meat. The gnome smiled and pointed to the front door, which stood open to the forest.

Bird song tempted the listener's ear to follow the trail of its sound, but his eyes stopped on the moon carving on the front door. Nodding to the gnome, he made his way to the front door and ran his hands along the grains. Lifetimes of woodworking ran through his blood and just as he suspected, the door was made of Sycamore. He smiled and stepped out across the mossy threshold.

Before him stretched the heavens bedecked with stars in every direction – east, west, north, south, above, and below. The archangels nodded to him. Raphael stood in the east, with the morning star upon his brow. In the west, Gabriel's sword illuminated with the glitter of the evening star. In the south, Michael's lance pierced through the worlds, as Uriel in the north poured sacred verse from his mouth giving life to the infinite universe. The open door cast a trail across the heavens, binding the stars together in a tangible Milky Way. He took a step forward on this celestial causeway, descending down towards the Earth on the Vernal Equinox.

The Nile of the heavens thus touched the Nile of the Earth, and he slipped through the fold in the mirror between them. Beneath him, the sands were still warm from the day's sun. The desert stretched west before him as the house of his father stood pointing to Orion's belt. In the light of the moon, and the dark of the inner passage, he found himself at home. He had not bought a magazine.

# Yahweh was a Woman

Yahweh was a woman. Be wary where you drop this knowledge, for it has been buried under Jerusalem for thousands of years. She was the consort of Shiva, the seed and egg of the House of David. She danced a terribly gorgeous dance of love, seduction, and chaos that rendered worlds and severed nations, making the destruction of Troy and Hiroshima seem as if child's play. Her dance still puts nations to their knees. Solomon attempted to bury the secret in his seal, and the Templars found it. Not the Seal of Solomon, but Yahweh.

Can you listen with your heart? Stories guide you in, like a lighthouse, safely around the illusive rocks of the labyrinthine mysteries. A story told with woven words is crisp enough to carry mountains and flexible enough to change each time we listen to the words resounding within the confines of the mind. Limitless if the landscape of the mind is allowed to access the furthest infinite reaches of the universe. This is not deductive reasoning of romantic and post-industrial scientists and technical jargonists, for they would attempt to convince us that the world is flat. Not with true conviction that the earth is no longer a globe, but that the evidence as measureable by the intellect, simply seeks to crush the imagination into a flat plain that serves the soul upon a platter to the vultures of the world.

In that world, everything is binary speech, tangible or not, for what you see is what you get. The world is flat. There are no secret doors to the Garden of the Gods. There are no spirit songs to canoe across celestial waters. And, there are no minotaurs at the center of the labyrinth, waiting to take your head and devour you. That is if you cannot take theirs' first.

There are a thousand upon a thousand worlds, infinite doors, and Ports of Entry to access them all. Conductive reasoning is the current, the river that traverses them all. To become a bard is to become an instrument of the Divine, is to become an effective conductor, a vessel that reaches in between the worlds and draws the nodes closer together to activate the current. Metaphor and imagination are the language of the divine, and lest you forget, Yahweh was a woman.

# Greek

# Socrates Prison

She came first in what I thought was scarlet lingerie, wrapped around the confines of rational thought as her curves drew the Watcher's eyes off the road. His pragmatic and usually obedient hands dropped from the wheel. He crashed into a forest of desire.

Her breasts were screaming to be tousled by tongue and teased with teeth. Her yoni was breathing steam and was saturated with longing.

Then, she pulsed in the current where the heat and cold swirl on stone, gyrating, undulating on the table of knowledge, and leapt on the Philosopher with a passion and tore off his head. She turns, smiling, crouched over his dead body with his fresh blood running down her neck and across her breasts.

She is covered in the scarlet lingerie of his blood, yet my desire is no less thwarted.

"You can have me," says I, "but not as prey, for I will throw you against mountain and the sea if I must. You will never hunger in my company."

Now she is my lover and teacher.

She is the Pythia and the voice of goddess. She is the passionate lover that inspires true wisdom and powerful inspiration. Go find a philosopher to feed to her if you must.

# Naiad's Cave

Well, this bag of plums should last me most of the day. I can trouble myself no more with the thoughts of how much of the juice will run down my tongue, or how much pulp will be all over my fingers and my chest. Let the stickiness prevail, for the plums of Skopelos are the next best thing that has been on my tongue yet in this life. I will not speak of what is the best, for that is between my lover and me.

A plum jumps in my mouth before I can get away from the farmer's stand. Oh my, these plums are feisty. Now, behave yourselves, you wild plums. How is a man supposed to get to the beach if plums keep jumping out of bags and hands, leaping into my mouth? The juice starts flowing over my tongue, and my knees get weak. The path before me becomes blurry momentarily and I stumble through the bush trying to find my way. Lo and behold, my feet irrevocably find the path again or a new path, and well, they all seem to be taking me to the shore to pray, so I guess there is not a lot to complain about, other than the bliss of heaven exploding upon my tongue and reminding me of my birthright.

ɔΨɕ

My back is pressed against the deck of a ship. I have been laying here in the sun, with oak and pine at my back for several moons, and my skin grows weary of Apollo's graces. Take me to the sea, Poseidon, take me into the deep and bring the cool darkness of the deep. Let me close my eyes and rest for a while.

ɔΨɕ

Boom-shalapa, boom-shalapa, boom shalapa...the sea is pounding the bedrock beneath me. Pray tell for what do the dwarves of the Aegean dig in the dark? Is it gold and marble, or do they simply yearn for dark respite from the prying fingers of Apollo? I do not know, but my eyelids become heavier, dreaming that the crashing of the sea against the cliffs beneath me is my lover's embrace.

Come to me, again and again. Bathe me in your passion, as I will rise to meet yours. Throw back the sheets, open the windows, and let the whole world hear our cries. Like water falling over a cliff, I step to the edge and dive over the precipice into the eternal blue heavens as below so above. Wrap me in your precious waters. I invite the waves to quicken, or to ebb and flow as the moon within you sees fit.

The crash of water upon my head wakes me to the moment. I swim quickly to the surface before I lose my breath and am drowned forever. Gasping for air, at the mercy of the persistent waves of the sea pulsing over my head, I find myself looking to the north, yet Apollo's chariot is already descending to the west and my face is no longer tortured by his embrace. I turn in the water, still bobbing on the pulsing waves beneath me. The cliff that I had somehow dove from in my sleep, stretched at least fifteen meters above the surface of the sea towards the ledge of pines upon which I slept.

Released from the bondage of unblemished sleep, a low sea cave looms before me. The waves of the sea are exploding through the entrance and slapping against the polished stone ceiling within, again and again. Oh, yes! Here I come! I see an invitation and I will swim into it, for the threads of Ariadne become tangible invitations begging to be tracked.

Oh, to drink of the divine nectar, and to stumble so freely upon yet another portal. Sail this ship through trepid waters and find port in the pulse of a lover's cave. Let me try my hand at swimming, or singing, but do not let me taste pure water and then tell me that it is not free. For freedom is the gift of the divine and I come to reclaim that right here and now.

So let me bow my head, as I wait outside of the entrance to your inner world. Let me stoop down and find the moving sand beneath the waves with my feet, touching the ripples with my toes as I gaze upon this splendor that unfolds before me. I reach out with my fingertips, and reverently touch the lips of the mouth of the cave, entering slowly, as I listen to the crush and slapping of each wave within.

Water, warm and clear, I am half floating, half planted in the sand, as I am sensually lifted with each wave and pushed deeper and deeper within. There is no going back, for she has called me into her inner chamber. She comes to me in the Aegean blue, transparent beyond all measure, yet with rich, limestone-green eyes that seem to float on the ceiling of the cave, reflecting the light of through pure salt water. She slaps at my chest with long fingers, white as a summer cloud, and she sighs as the water recedes through the rock and sand.

Poseidon weighs anchor outside of the cave and begins to sing. At first, his voice comes like thunder against the cliffs, and then it mellows into a steady drizzle. The raindrops mix with the saltwater dripping from the ceiling into my mouth.

"Milia, my lover, your father's voice stitches the worlds together as one."

ꝺΨꞓ

This is the way of things, when ripe fruit is eaten properly. When a paved path is left behind and bare feet find naked earth and rock. I look to the heavens from a perch on top of the cliffs, nestled in the crook of an arm of a curved pine. Sea birds circle the blue sky, enough so that I can see they are tracing the edges of my lover's summer skirt. Take me to the edge, I am diving in for another round.

# The Bus Station at Delphi

"Excuse me; is this the bus to Mt. Olympus?"

The hunch-backed bus driver just sat there. He did not look at me, nor emote any sort of sound to acknowledge my inquiry. He just sat there staring at the road ahead of him. I shuffled my backpack as it was getting heavy.

"Excuse me, mister bus driver; is this the bus to Mt. Olympus?"

He slowly turned to look at me. I could not tell if it was just the lighting or perhaps that I was exhausted, but he looked more like a goat than a man. He still said nothing. He stared at me as if I were a blackberry thicket and pointed to the sign above his head that showed the bus route. Yes, this seemed to be the route, though the southwest pass of Mount Parnassus where I was currently standing was not indicated on his route map. Figures as much and I had to give it to the fellow, I was not speaking Greek, though he did really look like a goat.

ɔΨc

I clearly recall the sound of their collar bells tinkling as they walked about the lower slopes of Mount Parnassus and in the pine-covered hills of the village of Kroki. The goats were the only thing resembling time for me, as their bells kept an unsteady beat that announced their every movement and whereabouts. Not that it mattered much, as those tinkling bells would have been making those same sounds 3,000 years ago.

The only thing that really seemed to keep time was the pulse in my veins. And try as I would to stay in the twenty-first century, or whatever century I had supposedly started this current incarnation in, I simply could not keep a proper time line under my belt. Eventually, I cast the belt off as it was too restricting in the dry heat of Aetolia anyway. It was better to let the sun kiss me, and the nymphs hamper my trajectory for the day, then to be tied up in knots of time and suffering.

A spring at the top of the ridge over the Pythia's oratory kept my mouth wet and my water bottle true to its name, otherwise it would have been an air bottle, and it would have been senseless to hold onto that as there was plenty of air around me. Carrying air in a bottle on this planet would have been as pointless as trying to keep time under my belt. So, I made sure that the spring and I were good friends and could find one another, even in the largest crowd.

Now, do not get me wrong, there was a massive crowd on the mountain. Heaven knows how long it takes to wait in line behind a bunch of pine trees and scrub oaks when you are trying to find your spring, especially when the trees are so old that their roots are knobby and you must follow the goats to get from one end of the valley to the other. Those are lines I can simply do without.

However, I did not mind waiting to see Pan, for he was hanging out in his cave facing west to the main ridge of Mount Parnassus. There was plenty of sun and interesting folks to converse with. Fortunately, most of the beings there spoke Hebrew and Aramaic, so I could navigate my way amongst the crowd with some semblance of decency. I did manage to step on the feet of a German giant at one point, but after a few heated words were exchanged, I managed to escape a tragic end by giving him the crown to Sicily. That seemed to appease him, and besides, Malta was enough of a headache for me as it was. So, in hindsight, I went back and gave him the crown of Malta as well. I would rather hangout on the Isle of Mann or Iona anyway for it is more to my temperament and climatic preference. Plus, I do not have to worry on those isles about Atlantians and Cretins interrupting my night songs among the standing stones, as they tend to do throughout the Mediterranean and Aegean.

Pan's cave was fascinating. It was massive, like the mull of a great sea beast, filled with many teeth of stone. In the center of the cave, a medium sized fire illuminated the main room, but only enough to make the shadows loom over me and make me feel small. Pan was

165

smaller than I expected, but no less impressive. He was seeing to the ministration of several ladies' personal needs while he spoke to me.

It is easy to assume that we know what a divine presence would speak to us, when we cross their path. Yet, it is difficult to imagine the impact that this presence creates in our lives. For in divinity lies a key to unmanifest reality. Like a space port or train station, we are propelled down pathways that are unforeseen and unpredictable. They set us upon a path that brings us to the door of some mystery that we have to knock on loudly, and say, "open, please!"

So I pushed aside the beaded curtains and passed the lovers in their sheets, and stepped out onto the landing pad. Not every ship is built the same, but the ports of Greece are sure to grant access to about any star system in a matter of moments. Prices have gone down too in recent centuries, so it is just a matter of getting there.

I tied my knapsack to my back and climbed onboard the nearest vessel to the Pleiades. Ten minutes later I was offshore and cruising along the sprouted stem of an Angel root plant through the stratosphere. The star-people fascinate me, as they are so old, yet seem so young. I have to wonder, as I walk the streets of interstellar space ports, why so many of the star-people find their feet walking next to mine. I love them so! All I can do is make a little nest for them on any of the varying continents on earth, so that when they come to visit me, they have a lovely place to feel comfortable and at home.

The main objective of these work trips to interstellar ports is to keep the trade routes between celestial beings open for commerce and dialogue. The majority of my home planet's ports are often under duress due to the isolation of Earth from much of the cosmos. It is easy too to forget about Earth unless ambassadors keep the dialogue harmonious between the heavenly bodies. The more trips that we make, the easier it is to keep the routes open. It often can be as simple as supply and demand, for if no one is making a particular trip, the companies that run the routes may cancel or change the route entirely in order to stay in operation. An entire port may move in an instant, leaving us scrambling to find public transportation to another Port of Entry.

So, I am honored to have left my belt with Pan at Parnassus. It is easier to wear the belt of Orion anyway, as by the time summer rolls around; I do not want to wear a belt or anything at all if I can. My clothing traps me in time, so I will wear it when I must go to Versailles to meet with the queen, or Cahokia to sit with the chief priest, but otherwise it is much more efficient to slide out of my clothing and skin, and drop into the various ports where people are expecting me and set about doing what I do when arrive.

It seems that most of the time when I arrive at a given location, everyone needs a density reminder. That somehow a part of them is eternal yet trapped in some limited biological vehicle. That is fine, rudimentary in fact, but the best tool for transmitting information or piloting interstellar travel is to either enter a quasar through a cognizance port, or to simply surrender any premonition or body of knowledge to the majesty of creation and the current that many have come to know as love. Love is the ticket to timelessness and the portal to interstellar travel through all time.

So get your tickets! They are free and available at just about any port in the universe. Avatars are often an excellent place to start, though there are many other routes that lead to a similar queue. I did mention that sometimes ports move. This is crucial, for if we hold onto the idea that a particular port is always going to be found in the same place or in the same biological being, we may find ourselves disappointed one day when we arrive at the station and see a closed sign, or see that it has been demolished and a fast food restaurant is being built in its place.

So let's hitch a ride back out to the Pleiadian station again. We have quite a few visitors from this star group that walk among us now on planet Earth, and I often come here to see if I can determine what it is that they see is so important as to travel repeatedly to our little star in our remote cul-de-sac of the Milky Way. They certainly are not after our technology, our nymphs, or our organs for experimentation. It seems that they have been coming here throughout our history and have imparted us with specific catalysts to seed chemical reactions in our minds. These catalysts or quasar seeds often end up fueling revolutions, kick-starting religious movements, and awakening untimely technologies.

Looking around the station, I see many who are dressed in white. They are crowded outside of a home where a visitor from another star system is teaching travelers how to more efficiently move through the worlds. Traveling at the speed of light is easy enough, but to retain all consciousness at each embodiment is not often an easy task unless the landing vessel is well tended too, and the pilot is well rehearsed on the route. Being that time is not an issue during interstellar travel, it is also imperative that upon arrival, some semblance of local time is adhered too, otherwise the tendency is for crucifixion, martyrdom of the visitor, or the opposite, for the visitor to grow hungry for temporal conquest and power. Remaining a Gnostic keeps one out of harms reach in most star systems.

I have made it to a few meetings of the Galactic Council. Most of the time the meetings are in silence. It is a white silence that is also a noise like a great wind or like stars imploding or being born again. The council members vary, depending on who can make it, but the resonant fact remains the same: let the play of consciousness continue through all of time. Let the celestial conductor direct the music. Perhaps the angels and demons can war over right and wrong, but the waves of entropy and order, will always cancel one another out, just as the human breath. The joy is in the rediscovery, the fulfillment of simple tasks, and alleviating the suffering of others. When the vessel that carries us falls away, suffering only brings our attention to the places where we have been distracted from communicating that which is eternal within.

ɔΨc

## Ports of Entry

So, I find myself at the bus station at a Port of Entry. I only have a few minutes to spare for offering my gratitude for the splendid hike around Parnassus and the cosmos. It was enough to recognize that it was time to move on, for I had business at Mount Olympus with the Argentineans and French. Somehow it had something to do with the inquisition and the Spaniards. The Teutons had the Grail stowed in the back of a truck heading to Polmaria, so we were safe for the time being. Either way, until next time we meet, I will see you at the crack of dawn, sliding between the sun and the earth.

# Contemporary American

# Headwaters

The Headwaters is a beginning place, where dreams and fireflies bridge the synapses of the mind. The water is sweet, and the forest is deep – always slumbering yet eternally awake. Walk warily amongst those forested slopes, for one may find they are forged in dragon's fires, and shaped under immortal elven hammers. Wear a fine helm of gold, polished to brilliance. Do not wear shoes. The unseen ones often speak softly in tongues that only the bottoms of feet will hear. Dress lightly, but well armored, for thorn and wood nettle will pierce your skin insistently until you give into the deep forest madness.

Walk warily amongst the forested slopes; rock strewn seeps and springs; and, under pine and oak crested ridges, for you will never walk alone. Wind your way among the mosses, orchids, and ferns, or let your shins brush trillium and larkspur so the pollen dusts the tops of your bare feet. Elven-kind will spring forth from fairy bells, bloodroot, and spring beauties, while dwarves creep to the edges of vision from granite outcrops and boulder fields strewn about by giants of old. Under the apple and elm, skyclad dryads wake the senses with the brushing of cinnamon fern fronds, a sip of sugar maple sap, and the scent of basswood flowers hanging heavily in their hair.

Come then to a garden. Here the elfin will not hide when you turn your head. With radiant smiles that seem to emanate star dust, they will welcome you deeper within the garden. Follow the boardwalk through the glen, for maidenhair ferns are sensitive to heavy feet, and the mosses and phosphorescent fungi are delicate to the touch. Watch attentively as heavy fog settles down into the rich cove from the ridges all around. Unwind your earthly cares and let friends share their warm hospitality and hearth.

Peter will greet you at the door to his cottage with a warm and knowing smile.

"Good to see you again," says he.

I pray that you will remember your manners and acknowledge his forthrightness, for it is likely that you have met before. In other worlds, this cottage and garden have been the center of a heated field of combat between varying forces of darkness and light. For now, it is a quiet cottage of the Fae, and Peter is their king. He will invite you in, that is, if you did not step on any ferns on the way. The elfin may wait outside, or they may join you within.

A hurdy-gurdy sits against the simple hearth. Peter will follow your gaze and invite you to play. A little lesson from the king himself is not a poor choice, for he will crank the most delicious sounds out of the old song box. Squeeze and whirl across the buzzing bridge of music until you are lost in the soundscape on the other side. Perhaps he will place the instrument into your hands and ask you to play the song to bring everyone back home. Allow your trials and tribulations to fall away as the elfin-kind are mesmerized, then distracted as you begin to doubt yourself. Unleash yourself into the music until your confidence is renewed, and the elfin are filled with a fiery wildness.

Play, and play with wild abandon. Do not worry if the power and majesty you invoke disturbs the electronic giants and overlords. They may alert the military drones to the omniscient power of your making, but fear not. Let them open their guerilla assault upon the Elfin yet again as they have for centuries.

Do not stop playing! Play until the hurdy-gurdy becomes an instrument of illusion and entices the mechanized invaders into the crack between the worlds. The host of the Otherworld is like a living wall of spring, both permeable and complete. Flowers and plants will unfold and pour forth like lake water behind a collapsing dam, rushing down the mountains to engulf steel and flame. Some of the strangest projections of the Otherworld will rise in mass. Earth giants, covered in vines, flowers, and showers of glowing mycorrhizae will pour down the mountain followed by a cavalry of flowers blooming within flowers, over and over like miniature supernova, riding in rank on the backs of grape vines and Dutchman's pipes.

Green women will morph into flowers and herbs, yet will melt into the rolling mass of the Elfin pouring down the slopes. Some of the riders in that wave will retain individual faces, looking sadly on at the fated invaders as they are enveloped and disappear from this world. Allies of the Elfin simply are rolled into the wave and disappear as well. The invading force will skirmish with technical firepower and other devices of destructive intent to keep the wave at bay, but it will do nothing to thwart the wave of Elfin defenses.

Keep playing that hurdy-gurdy until Peter offers to take over for you. Then, stand and let the wave roll over you as well. Relinquish your fears. The wave will not hurt or destroy you. It will wash over you and your kin like a gentle warm waterfall, followed by a late summer breeze coursing across a field of ripe barley. The ripe grains and grass blades will caress you. So prepare to leave the thick layers of clothing behind, for the nettles are long gone. Relax and enjoy your time walking slowly in the Blessed Realm.

You may find yourself wander into a waiting area, not much unlike a classic train station, minus the clock and any sense of urgency. You will notice that there are lines forming for those who are also appearing in the station. Go ahead and get in a queue. This is the Otherworld's gold exchange. When the Elfin are not in the time-cloaks that they wear in the world we humans inhabit most frequently, they often appear very similar to *homo sapiens*. Depending on what their deeds were in our world, or as some call Middle Earth, they will receive their due payment in gold.

So get in line! See what it is that you can be paid while you are there. Perhaps you can trade it in for some valuable skill, like how to fly, or to heal the sick, or give sight to the blind. Perhaps you can trade in and learn how to be a dream caster. Teach others how to fly, change shape, or levitate...all the while, the vigilant bells of the station are whispering:

"It's all a dream....

It's        all        a        dream....

# Trading Eyes

He watched the three women walking up the steel stairs of the fire escape with little more than a curiosity. They were all beautiful in their own way, but the sound of their high heeled shoes on the steel was more alluring to him in the moment. The pattern was irregular. Sometimes the rhythm staccato, sometimes complete chaos, as they struggled to look smooth and sultry, while fumbling on a rough surface with unsuitable shoes. Opening the door on the second floor to the loft, the last one, the one with the brunette bob-cut and the sharp facial features turned and gave him an inviting wink.

He smiled and the sky lit up in fiery pink and salmon. For a moment he closed his eyes, and then opened them again to see the first hints of sunrise through the turkey oaks and loblolly pine. His pillow was pressed against the headboard, so he dragged it down under his head. Lying on his belly, with his head in the south, the first colors of the dawn warmed the eastern window. Outside, the surf washed across pink sands and deposited the morning's collection of mollusk shells on the shore.

"It is truly a gift to be alive," he thought. "It is gift to merely be here and to be able to feel so much gratitude for this life that I have lived fully."

He lay there with his head on the pillow and his face towards the east waiting. For what comes next is one of the most magical moments that any being can ever experience in life. As he lay there, allowing his eyes to open and close as they will, drifting between lucid dreams and waking consciousness, the sun emerged from the sea and sent a wave of golden light across the gap between them, and landed ever so gently upon his face and pillow. He smiled again. Closing his eyes as not to be blinded, he let the sun warm and soften his skin. Outside, the surf shifting the sand soothed his ears while a few tears welled in the corners of his eyes and trolled down his cheek to his pillow, and he fell back asleep.

ɔΨϾ

She invited him in the back door because it was easier to sneak into her loft that way. When her parents were away for church meetings on Wednesday nights, it was the only way he could spend precious time with her on a weeknight. Her parents were still pretty old-fashioned and only wanted them to see one another after church on Sundays. He liked coming in the back door. There was a rebellious power that surged through him, especially in the evasion of the looming feeling that someday they would be caught. And the antique back door was dark green, his favorite color. The paint on the door looked like wax, from layer upon layer over the past few centuries. After coming inside, he sat down in the living room and she collapsed into his arms, wrapping her arms around him and running her fingers up the spine of his neck.

ɔΨϾ

He woke up and smiled, for the sun was sitting a few degrees higher above the sea now. Rubbing his eyes to push back the castings of the Sandman and his dried tears, he stretched slowly. His bones and sinew slowly popping back into the comfortable place that ninety years of shuffling around the Earth had come to know. Whether it was his mind that shaped his posture, or his posture that shaped his mind, he was not sure and no longer cared. That sort of thing was for younger folks to consider. He would get out of bed now, or at least that was his intention. The sound of the surf below his balcony was inviting him to his daily walk. The sound of the surf was calling.

ɔΨϾ

When the phone rang, it ripped him from his sleep again. He jumped up off the couch, his book falling to the floor and his coffee mug spilling across the jarred coffee table. He was disoriented for a moment and it took him a moment to recognize his home. The phone screamed at him again. Outside, the city was bustling with the sounds of commerce and midday traffic.

"Ok, ok. I am coming," he said.

The phone rang again as he wound his way around the coffee table into the kitchen. He picked up the phone.

"Hello?"

He began unwinding the long cord so he could clean up the coffee while he took the call.

It was her. She had gone to Berlin on business earlier in the week and was temporarily trapped there. It sounded like the Russians were demanding all flights from Berlin be stopped until some compromise could be made with the Americans. His stomach turned and his chest tightened.

"I knew this trip was a bad idea. What if something happens to you? Oh, honey! When can you come home?"

The phone line was disconnected and all he could hear was the incessant beeping of the lost call blaring at him through the ear piece.

ɘΨɔ

His eyes cracked open abruptly. He must have fallen asleep again in the brilliance of sunrise. His alarm was beeping incessantly, demanding that it was time to get out of bed. The sun was again a few degrees higher in the eastern sky than when he had fallen back asleep. Down on the shore, the tide was receding further back from the dunes. Waxing moon tides such as these were always hissing at him to come walking much earlier in the day. If he wanted to find any whelks or other unique seashells on his walk, he needed to get moving.

He sat up and slowly got out of bed, while simultaneously pulling the sheets and covers up toward the pillow as his mother had taught him as a boy. He was certain she learned that from her mother and her from her mother, and so on, back across the hills of Ireland since before the morning Saint Patrick set foot on that green isle. Making his way to the bathroom, he was grateful to still be on his own at this age. To go to the bathroom, to brush his teeth, to feed himself; these are things that most people take for granted.

The unseasonal warm air greeted him as he stepped onto the beach. The purring of the sea as it sifted through the sands invited him to take a deep breath, turn toward the sun, and close his eyes.

ɔѰɕ

There she was. Her long brown hair cascaded down across her chest as she pushed her small framed glasses deeper onto her nose. She was reading from a book to a younger woman, whose attention was fully focused on the cards laid out on the Mexican blanket in the meadow. He walked toward her. When she looked up, he could see the sun in her eyes. It was almost as if laughter lived there and could not be asked to reside anywhere else. The rusty-brown Volkswagen bus at her back was filled with blankets and coolers.

"I know you," she said.

She stood, stepped towards him, and took his hands in hers. They looked into one another's eyes for a moment as memories unfolded between them that he was certain had never been shared between them. He did not even know her name, yet memories that neither of them had shared in this life danced through his mind. He pulled her closer and she wrapped her arms around his waist and pressed her cheek into his chest. He could feel the warmth of her breath through his shirt. Her hands on the small of his back fit perfectly and seemed to speak a language that he remotely recalled from his childhood. And he surrendered, pulling her closer.

ɔѰɕ

The sea gulls called overhead and pulled him from his revere. Taking his hat off, he blinked in the morning sunlight and scratched

180

his grey hair before placing the wide-brimmed cap back on his head. Looking south then north, he was resolved to walk north along the shore this morning. He set a steady pace for a gentleman who has been here for almost a century. One could almost imagine him marching with the military, either on rounds or in a formal parade. His steps were snappy, but not overtly heavy. With the receding tide, the sands were compact so he hardly left a footprint.

With the sun on his right cheek, he began his brisk five-mile walk. The sound of the gulls and the surf, mixed with the sun and gentle breeze were the necessary ingredients for an unspoiled morning.

ɔΨc

The doorbell rang and the children jumped up from underneath the Christmas tree and ran to the door shouting.

"Grandma! Grandma! Grandma!"

Before he could get up from the leather couch, the door was thrown open, and his mom and dad came tramping in the front door. Snow was flying everywhere and the children were full of laughter and now wet feet.

His mom set down her Christmas gifts and the pies that she had brought with her and gathered all of her grandchildren in an enormous hug. He remembered when his mother used to hug him and his siblings like that. The feeling was somewhere between having the loveliest blanket wrapped around you - a homemade quilt at that - laden with the unique scents of his mother's home. The old oak arms seemed to stretch for miles and banished any feeling of darkness or wrong to the furthest corners of the universe.

And on mornings like this, when all the children's cares in the world were thrown out the door, a few wet feet and splashing of snow could do nothing to bend the fates' wishes. Grandfather let out his first roaring joke of the morning, clearing the house of any stoic cobwebs, and leaving his son rolling his eyes, as he squeezed all of the air out of him in a massive bear hug.

ꙩΨꙅ

Now that is how you hug someone you love, he thought. Slowing down his pace along the shore, he stooped to pick up a shell. The colors were outstanding. It was by no means a perfectly intact whelk, but it was gorgeous beyond all means. The top was almost intact, and the spiral seemed almost like an invitation to walk down them, like a spiral staircase, and to pull a bottle of wine out of the cellar to share with loved ones on a cold winter's night.

Chuckling to himself, he bent back down and pressed the whelk into the sand so that only the top showed. Perhaps a child would find it just like that before the tide came in much further, or perhaps people half his age riding around on the beach in a golf cart would run over it and change its shape again. It did not matter. It was simply an idea, an invitation.

In the distance, he could see someone dancing on the shore, or so it appeared from his vantage as he walked toward them. The movements embraced both the sun and shadow, almost as if the dancer was inviting the morning sun to join in the fun. The edges of the dancer were obscured by the morning breeze bending sand snakes across the beach. The gentleman shielded the right side of his face with his hands, to reduce the glare of the morning sun and the sting of blowing sand upon his cheeks. He tried to focus his eyes through the split between his ring and pinky fingers, but the elements and sounds around him were obscured by the burning sands.

ꙩΨꙅ

The flamingos were upset from their fishing in the mudflats and rose up with squalor to the tops of the mangroves. Another tourist boat was motoring up the estuary to disturb the peace. He slipped into the recesses of the white mangroves to the brackish pools where she lay sleeping in a little sun spot. He let his eyes follow the lines of her limbs from head to foot. Her short, sandy hair was a mess from their mating. Her flat belly slowly rose and fell with each breath. Her legs dangled slightly over the edge of the hummock and her toes were just above the surface of the brackish water.

This is where life begins, he thought, as he watched the fish chasing juvenile shrimp amongst the roots of the mangroves, here where the mangroves play host to a thousand organisms. Where orchids cascade over the crotches of old trees, and ferns are large enough to sleep in. His tail curled around his mate's chest and his ears turned to the west again. The tourist boat was already leaving and she was stirring in her sleep.

ɔΨc

He shook his head and brought his eyes back into focus. The wind had died down and he no longer needed to protect his face from the bite of the sand. The dancer was still moving, but certainly this was not dancing. It seemed as if the movements were mimicking animals. At first he was a crane, then a tiger, and then something altogether the gentleman was completely unfamiliar with.

He reached into his shirt. For years he had kept her ring there on a thin silver chain. Touching the gold reminded him of the preciousness of life. The gulls seemed to be uninterested in following him any longer and now he had only the surf, the ring, and the shadow dancer.

The dancer stood in stillness, eyes closed, facing the sun.

"Ah," thought the gentleman, "he is doing the same thing as I. He is unwinding his thoughts to invoke the majesty of life. As death is ever at the door and shadows from the past or fantasy cause us to stumble over the threshold of what gifts lay at our feet in the present. Which world is reality, the discoloration of the present by the past, the constant struggle to fully catch up to the present and leave all history behind us, or the pining of future probabilities pulling on us like a spoiled child? I cannot hold onto one timeline more than the other, or waste time sorting out whose memories and dreams are whose. I am simply a witness to this remarkable creation."

The young man turned to the elder as he approached.

For a few long moments, their eyes met. One pair blurred with years, the other young with ambition, but both quiet and full of vision.

"When I saw the sun rise this morning, I did not look into the mirror until now," spoke the young man.

"Nor did I," spoke the elder.

Pulling a lock of hair out from in front of his face, the young man joined in step with the elder for a few paces.

"You keep a brisk pace, young sir," said the younger.

The elder smiled. Sometimes a simple compliment from another is enough to lift one above all the worries and cares of the world. Inside his chest, warmth grew from his heart that seeped into his entire being like warm tea. He did not need his coat anymore. He took it off and snapped it over his right shoulder with military precision, turning his head to the wind and continuing his brisk pace with a smile.

The younger slowed his pace, watching the sand pipers chasing insects and mollusks across the tide break. Several deer ran out over the dunes and jumped in the surf for a moment before disappearing back into the maritime scrub.

The elder too had touched him in a way that he had invoked through his dance of light and shadow. Grace washed over him like a warm summer breaker. He closed his eyes in gratitude and smiled as his mind opened to an ocean of possibility.

ɔΨɔ

He watched the three women walking up the steel stairs of the fire escape with little more than a curiosity. They were all beautiful in their own way, but the sound of their high heeled shoes on the steel was more alluring to him in the moment. The pattern was irregular. Sometimes the rhythm staccato, sometimes complete chaos, as they struggled to look smooth and sultry in front of him, while fumbling on a rough surface with unsuitable shoes. Opening the door on the second floor to the loft, the last one, the one with the long sandy-blond hair and radiant green eyes, turned and gave him an inviting wink.

*Jeremy Schewe*